Marching
As to War

JUSTIN WATSON

ISBN: **0991021215**
ISBN-13: **978-0991021215**

Difficulties are things that show what men are.
- Epictetus, *The Discourses, 1.24*

1

The girl walked out of the darkness into the light of our fire. Wet and cold after a long patrol in the rain, we sat close to the flames. None of us said much. Too much effort to talk. That was when we saw the girl.

It took a moment to realize she was not a man. She didn't dress as our mountain girls did in those days, with unshorn hair and a long skirt. Instead, her hair was chopped short, and she wore a man's hat, coat, shirt, and britches. She also carried a rifle. It lay cradled in the crook of her left arm like a sleeping child.

We all rose to our feet. I don't know why. Perhaps even then we sensed a power in her. She said nothing. An old man came up and stood behind her, just visible in the light of the fire. He asked for the commanding officer. No one answered. Finally, I pointed up the hill and said, "Captain's up yonder."

The man thanked me and began to walk that way. He moved slowly with a bad limp. But the girl stood and looked at me. The fire reflected in her eyes. She nodded to me and then moved into the dark, toward the Captain's tent.

That is how I met the girl. I didn't know anything had changed even though everything had. I only felt uneasy.

I'm telling this story because I'm the only one who can. I'm the only one left. Many of our people think they know all about her and the war against the Government. But they weren't there at the beginning. I was. And they weren't there at the end. I was.

You may not like, or even believe, what I have to say. So be it. All I ask is you hear me out before you decide.

2

The next morning I had the dream, the bad one. Like always, I came awake and sat bolt upright, breathing hard, full of anger, fear, and shame.

The dream was of the first man I ever killed. It was on a real foggy day. My squad stumbled across some raiders--just ran into them where two trails crossed. One of them jumped on me before I could get my rifle up. He and I rolled around wrestling, gouging, and biting, each trying to get a knee in the other's balls. I remember he had sharp blue eyes, a neatly trimmed graying mustache, and a missing tooth in front.

It went on and on until I reached some place beyond rage and got my hands around his throat. I beat his head against a rock. I didn't stop when he went limp. Did not stop until his head cracked.

I would always wake from the dream at the crack. The dream was bad, but the real thing had been worse. I lay with my face in the dirt, coughing and gasping for air. My heart was beating so hard I was afraid something might tear loose. It took me a long time to stop shaking. Then I had to go through his pockets for anything useful--food, a knife, bullets--but they were empty. I pulled off his boots but gave them away. Too big. So all I got from him was the dream. Awake, I never thought of him, but the blue-eyed man came almost every time I slept.

I got up and got busy with chores--airing my bedroll, relieving myself, gathering some wood, getting some tea and bread. After that, I felt better, but I had time on my hands, nothing to do until our patrol went out late in the afternoon. So I sat at the fire with the rest of my squad.

Stokes was cleaning his rifle. Harris was sewing a patch on his coat. We called him "the boy," because he had only been in the militia a few weeks. Riley was still asleep, snoring softly. Weber had gone to his sister's wedding more than a week before. We expected him back soon, but it would be no surprise if he stayed up home. Sad to say, lots of us were doing that--deserting--in those days.

I got out a pencil stub and some paper I found in an abandoned house. The paper was yellow with age, but I was glad to have it. Since the Plague, of course, anything for writing had become rare. I planned to write a letter. In those days, we would send a letter along with a traveler, who would carry it as far as he might and then pass it along to someone going closer. This worked better than you would expect so long as you weren't in a hurry.

The letter was to Maggie. She and I were to be married next spring when my time in the militia was over. Maggie had been my older brother's wife, but when he had taken sick and died last year, a duty to marry her had passed to me. The Bible says in the twenty-fifth chapter of Deuteronomy,

> If brethren dwell together, and one of them die, and have no child, the wife of the dead shall not marry without unto a stranger: her husband's brother shall go in unto her, and take her to him and to wife, and perform the duty of an husband's brother unto her.

Now I didn't expect I would find a better wife than Maggie, not living where we did. Maggie was a good Christian--but not preachy or Jesusy, like a lot of girls. She was strong enough to bear many children and could even read and write. A rare thing among mountain girls. Everyone thought she was pretty. But I didn't know what she thought of me. She and my older brother had chosen one another. Now she was supposed to marry me. So it was hard to know what to say to her.

I had managed to put down "Dear Maggie," when Weber came walking up carrying his rifle and bedroll, a big grin on his face. He had come back after all.

"You boys miss me?" he said

"Hell no," Stokes said. "We was enjoying the peace and quiet."

"Glad to hear it," Weber said, dropping his things and sitting by the fire.

"How was the wedding?" I said.

Weber grinned and started telling us what a fine time he had had. He told us about all the eating, dancing, and whiskey drinking he had done. Weber tended to stretch the truth a little, but I still enjoyed hearing it.

When Weber was done, Harris said, "Did you hear anything . . . you know . . . news?"

In those days, the only news you got was what a traveler heard from other travelers.

Weber's grin went away. "Yeah, I heard something. A feller at the wedding, name of Baines, told me a story. My Uncle Earl found him, sick and near starved, took him in. Baines said he was from up in the Shenandoah. The Government's army come to his town last year. And yeah, they had machine guns and the trucks like we heard about."

"Damn," Stokes said. "How many soldiers was there?"

Weber shrugged. "Baines didn't say, but there was enough so that nobody tried fighting. The soldiers just rode in one day and took over. He said the head officer got everybody together and made a speech about how they was part of the Restored United States of America now. The soldiers put up the old flag, and the officer said everybody had to swear an oath to obey the Government. But one man refused."

"Why?" Harris said.

"Don't know," Weber said. "Anyway, some soldiers grabbed him, beat him up some, and dragged him over to the officer. And when the man still refused to swear, the officer took out a pistol and shot him in the head."

We all were silent until Harris said, "You're shitting me."

Weber shook his head. "Baines said after that everybody swore and was damn quick about it. Then the soldiers started going in the houses and taking any guns--"

"Took their guns?" Harris said. "How they expect people to put meat on the table? Protect themselves?"

"Reckon they didn't much care," Weber said. "Anyway, Baines said the soldiers also closed down the churches, said they had to apply for a license from the Government. When some folks commenced having church at home, the soldiers took them off in trucks. And they--"

"And they never came back?" I said.

Weber nodded. "Baines heard a rumor the soldiers were going to put all the young men in the Army. So he decided to sneak away and go to some kin he had down here. Couldn't use the roads cause he didn't have no government pass. Had to go cross-country and he got lost, real bad lost. That's when Uncle Earl found him."

"How you know this Baines was telling the truth?" Harris said.

"Don't know. Not for a fact," Weber said. "But he sure looked scared talking about it. I didn't take him for no liar."

"I don't know," Stokes said. "People tell stories. Take a little thing and make it big."

"I believe it," I said. "What the soldiers did only makes sense."

"Sense?" Stokes said. "Sounds just plain crazy mean to me."

"No," I said. "It makes sense because it's crazy mean. They want to keep people scared. Keep them from fighting back." I could have told them things I read in old history books about what some governments used to do. But the boys always thought I was just showing off with book talk. They got my meaning. No need to say more.

"Yeah," Harris said, "but my Grandpa told me the old Government couldn't do things like that. And it's the same government, the United States, ain't it?"

"No," I said. "Just men with guns telling other folks what to do. They call it Restored United States, so we'll think it's the same. The old flag is just a bright rag now. Don't mean a thing, boys."

"Here's what I want to know," Stokes said. "What's Winslow's boy gonna do about all this?"

In those days, "Winslow's boy," or "Little Charlie," was what we called Charles Winslow. When Reverend David Winslow died, the Council of Elders elected his son, Charles, as our leader.

Pretty much everything we had--everything good anyway--was David Winslow's doing. We thought about him like the Israelites must have thought of Moses. With that big beard of his, he even looked like one of the prophets in the old Bibles that had pictures.

At the time of the Plague, David Winslow was a preacher. But when he was young, he had been in the old Government's army. So he knew about fighting and he had organized our militia with ranks and discipline. But most important, he showed us how to live godly in an ungodly world. We followed the Commandments God laid down for His people in the Bible. Without God's law, Winslow always said, the law of darkness in men's hearts would destroy the world. And folks believed him because they had seen the Plague and what came after. They had seen that darkness with their own eyes. It was as real to them as the earth beneath their feet.

When I first joined the militia, David Winslow was still alive, and I heard him preach. Winslow's preaching wasn't windy like the sermons I had heard up home. He said things straight and plain, just the way Jesus did in the Bible. Not a wasted word. He would look out at us with those hard dark eyes of his and dare us to believe as much as he did. Then he would say a prayer, pick up his rifle, and go out on patrol with us.

But the son was not the father. From what we had heard, Charles Winslow stayed at the headquarters, what we called Central Camp, and was always having meetings. He never went out on patrol and always slept in a bed. It seemed he just left us to drift. And we drifted. I had seen the change in our men. More deserted or shirked their duty. More whiskey drinking. More sneaking away to go with whores in the towns.

"What do you expect Little Charlie to do?" Harris said. "Get us new rifles? Machine guns and trucks like the damn government soldiers? He can't."

"I know that," Stokes said.

"Then what can he do?" Harris said.

Stokes shrugged. "I just want him to tell us the truth. We hear these stories about the Government and all, but we don't hear a goddamn thing from him."

"Yeah," Weber said, "Charles Winslow's acting like he can't smell the shit in the outhouse."

After that, we all got quiet. Maybe there was some way to stop the

Government, even with their machine guns and trucks. Yet we wouldn't even try unless someone would lead us, someone who could make us believe again. I was tired of being afraid. I just wished David Winslow were still alive.

We all sat staring at fire until Weber said, "So what's been happening around here?"

I thought of the strange girl who had come into camp. But something in me didn't want to talk about her.

"Well," Harris said, "there was that girl."

"A girl? What girl?" Weber fancied himself a man of romantic charm. So talk of a girl in camp got his interest.

"Don't know," Stokes said, "Last night, she just walked up to our fire. An old man with her asked for the Captain."

Weber grinned. "What's she look like? Pretty?"

Harris and Stokes started laughing. I didn't.

"What's so damn funny?" Weber said.

"Yeah, she was real pretty." Harris said. Then he and Stokes laughed some more.

Weber scowled, getting angry. Stokes saw this and said, "She's dressed like a man."

Weber leaned forward. "Like a man?"

"Yep, in britches and boots like any of us," Harris said.

"And her hair was all chopped off," Stokes said.

"Had a rifle too," Harris said.

"How come?" Weber said. "What's she doing here?"

Stokes let out a little snort of laughter and said, "Maybe she's come to join the militia."

We all busted out laughing. Even me. In those days, we couldn't imagine a girl doing anything other than keeping house and raising children. Of course, I knew from old books that before the Plague women had done all sorts of men's work--even soldiering. Some folks said this was part of the wickedness of that time because it was against God's law. Some folks said this, but I didn't know what to believe. I just knew there had never been girls in our militia, and it seemed foolish to think that would ever change.

After we had stopped laughing, Weber rolled out his bedroll and stretched out, hoping for a little sleep. The rest of us drifted back to what we had been doing before. I picked up my letter and read the words, "Dear Maggie." I was chewing on my pencil stub, trying to think of something to write, when someone tapped me on the shoulder.

I looked up and saw Price, our squad leader. "Captain wants you," he said.

"Me?" I said. The other men looked at us, curious. When the Captain asked for a man, it usually meant trouble. But I hadn't done anything.

Nothing I could think of anyway.

"Yeah, you."

"What for?"

He shrugged.

Price didn't know or didn't care to tell me. So I put away the paper and pencil, got my rifle, and went up the hill.

The Captain was sitting outside his tent on an old stump, holding a pipe, and looking out over the valley to the endless ridges of mountains beyond. They were beautiful in the rising light of the day. It was that time in the spring when I was still surprised how everything had turned so green so quick. I could look at those mountain ridges until my eyes gave out, but I would never see it all. The Captain looked tired, like he had been up for days. It took a moment for him to notice me.

"Sir," I said, "you wanted me?"

He puffed on his pipe a little before answering. "You're gonna take our guest to Central Camp." He nodded toward the tent, where I could see the girl and the old man studying a map. The Captain handed me a piece of paper, my written orders to present at the camp, and then a sealed letter. He told me to give the letter to the officer on duty when I arrived. I put them in my coat.

"What about the man?" I said.

"That's her uncle. Got a bad leg. He won't be going with you. So you'll need a second man."

"Riley?"

"Good. Take Riley. Just keep him out of trouble."

"I will, Sir. But . . . why'd you pick me?"

He smiled. "She asked for you."

That made me curious. I looked over to the tent, but her back was to me.

"Sir, what's all this about?" I said.

"Don't you worry about that. Just get her there as soon as possible. I'll have her meet you and Riley at the western edge of camp."

I went down the hill and found Price. When I told him the Captain was sending Riley and me on special duty, he said, "Shit! Go on then, leave me even more short-handed."

"Hey Price," I said, "wasn't my idea. Take it up with the Captain."

Price just gave me a hard look and turned away, pissed off again. I was glad to be shut of him for a few days.

Riley was still sleeping in the morning sun, his hat down over his face.

"Wake up," I said, nudging him with a boot. "We got a special job."

Riley pushed up his hat and smiled. "Good. When?"

"Now."

"Even better." And he got to his feet and stretched like a big cat. I told him where to find the girl. I would hunt up some extra food and ammo and meet them there.

Weber had overheard. "The girl? What's going on?"

"Taking her to Central."

"Why? Who the hell is she?"

I just shrugged, gathered up my things, and headed off to scrounge up some food and ammo. When I was done, I found the three of them at the edge of camp. A few yards away from the girl and her uncle, Riley stood waiting. He had a sly smile, like something was funny. I was still looking at Riley, wondering what he was up to, when I realized the girl was standing not two feet in front of me. She wasn't tall, but she stood up straight and looked me right in the eye. Her hat was off, and I could see her hair looked goddamn awful, like she had hacked it off in a hurry with a dull knife. The britches she had on were far too big. The waist was cinched in by an old leather belt and the legs were rolled way up at the bottom. I wondered who had lent her those clothes. Maybe her uncle. To be honest, she was kind of funny looking.

"You a saved Christian?" she said.

"Yes, Ma'am," I said. Then I felt foolish. The girl was younger than me. But she had caught me by surprise.

"Keep the Commandments?"

"I do my best," I said, leaving off the Ma'am.

"How long you been in the militia?"

"Near three years."

"You read and write?" she said.

"Yeah."

"Good at it?"

"Good enough," I said, wondering how long this would go on.

"Let's go," she said and turned to her uncle, hugged him, and said something in his ear. He looked about to cry.

To give them a moment, Riley and I walked toward the woods. He said, "Ma'am?"

"Oh, never mind." I was a little angry about her questions.

"She did the same to me. Have to say I didn't do as well on the one about Commandments. But she didn't ask me about reading or writing. Wonder why."

"Maybe it's plain you're an ignorant Hillbilly."

"Maybe. But I reckon it's something about you."

3

Riley led the way through the woods. I brought up the rear. The girl walked between. After about two hours, we stopped for rest and water. The trail had been uphill. The girl was breathing hard but keeping up. She seemed anxious to move on. Then I took point, and we walked for another two hours before resting. We continued like this throughout the day, talking no more than what was necessary. The girl, for whatever reason, said nothing.

In the early afternoon, we crested a ridge and began moving downhill. It was almost dark when we got to where the trail flattened out and crossed an old blacktop road.

"Let's camp at the well," I said. We left the trail, walking a quarter mile up the road.

Riley and I had been here before. He knew why I liked the spot. There was an old car close to the well. The car was just a rusting hulk, a shell of what it had been. But I liked imagining what it had been like to drive such a car a mile a minute down big broad roads, listening to radio music. My parents and grandparents, of course, had told me about life before the Plague, when almost everybody had such a car, when it was easy to get plenty of food, and when you didn't have to carry a gun everywhere you went. I had also seen pictures in old books and magazines of all the nice things people had, the way they dressed, how happy and well fed everyone looked. Maybe life hadn't been that good but I liked to imagine that rusting old car when it was new, shiny, and full of power. It could have taken me anywhere I wanted to go.

We settled in, filled our canteens, built a fire, and ate. Riley and I had traveled together so long that it was as easy to be quiet as to speak. But the girl upset our balance. It isn't like she did anything. She just sat staring into the fire, drinking some water, eating jerky. She hadn't said a word since morning. Yet her silence, and our questions about her, made us fill the time with talk.

"Still gonna fix up that old car?" Riley said. It was one of our running jokes.

"Oh yeah," I said, playing along, "all I need are a few parts, some fuel, maybe a coat of paint."

"And some oil? Might be kinda rusty after all these years."

"Sure, some oil. Thanks for the reminder."

The girl was looking at me, puzzled. "You talking about that old heap of rust?"

"Just joking," I said.

She looked like she didn't get the joke.

"Well," I said, not sure how to explain. "I'm interested in things from the time before, like that car. Riley thinks that's foolish. He thinks--"

"Gone for good," he said. "Can't bring all that back. Best forget it."

"Come on," I said. "They knew so much back then. They could do so much. They even--"

"I know, I know. They even sent men to the moon. But what good did that do them? Didn't stop the Plague. Didn't stop everything from going to hell after, did it?"

"Yeah, but--"

"The Plague was God's punishment," the girl said. "Nothing could stop that."

Riley and I looked at each other. Of course, we had heard people say the Plague was God's punishment. My Grandpa used to say that.

"Now the way I heard it," I said, "the old Government had made the disease as a weapon against its enemies. The disease got loose somehow and spread."

My parents told me it was early June when people began dying--first dozens, then hundreds, then thousands. Then the sickness was everywhere, and nobody bothered to keep count anymore, or even bury the dead. Bodies rotted where they fell. Everything stopped. The electricity and telephones went off. The water pipes went dry. Soon there was no fuel for the cars and no food in the stores. Some of the survivors began to take what they needed, and then to steal what they wanted. Before long, gangs of men roamed like packs of wild dogs. No one could stop them. By the end of that summer, the old government had disappeared just like the electricity and the water. In the Book of Judges, the Bible says, "In those days there was no king in Israel: every man did that which was right in his own eyes." So it was after the Plague.

"That's what I heard too," Riley said. "An accident."

"That's how it happened," she said, "but not why."

"OK. Why?" I said.

"Pride," she said. "We was too proud of our cars, the moon, and all the rest of it. And in our pride, we turned from God. So God punished us, humbled us, with the Plague."

When I was a child, I was always frightened when Grandpa talked about God this way. So frightened, I could barely breathe. I was frightened of disease and death, of course, but I was more frightened of a God who would punish and kill so many people. It made all the talk of God loving and forgiving us into the biggest lie there could be.

She looked at us without blinking. She was either dead sure of herself, or plain crazy. Maybe both.

"Just who the hell are you, anyway?" I said.

"Jane Darcy. I have a message for Charles Winslow. The Lord has laid it upon me to save our people."

Riley let out a low whistle. Then he said, "God talks you often, does he?"

"Not often. But enough."

Riley leaned back a little and looked over at me, his eyebrows up. He seemed to be saying, Your turn.

"Save us?" I said. "Save us from what?"

"The Government," she said. "The Restored Government of the United States of America." She said it slow.

"Just how you gonna do that?"

"Lead our men into battle."

"Ever been shot at?"

"No."

"Can you use that rifle?"

"Some."

I looked over at Riley. He smiled. I turned back to her and said. "So if you lead our men against the Government army, what then?"

She looked at me as if I had asked if it got dark after the sun went down. "Then God will give us victory."

For a long moment, we were silent. The only sounds were the crackling of the fire and the hum of bugs out in the woods. I looked over at Riley. He wasn't smiling anymore. The girl put away her food and canteen. She lay down, turned from us, and pulled up her blanket. We sat looking at her back. After a while, Riley stood up and said he would take first watch.

There was nothing for me to do but sleep. But I couldn't. "The Lord has laid it upon me," she had said. Craziness, I thought, pure craziness. To my way of thinking, God might want a thing but we had no way of knowing what. He didn't tell people things. Not anymore. All we could do was try to remember what the Bible says, use common sense, and do our best. I would fight the Government if it came into our mountains. I don't know if God wanted that or not. But I would fight all the same.

I gave up trying to sleep and went over to where Riley sat, keeping watch.

"Sorry, I got you into this," I said. "I didn't know she was crazy."

He didn't answer right away. Instead, he leaned his rifle against a tree and scratched his beard. I had learned to listen when Riley took time to think.

"No need to be sorry," he said. "What she says is sure enough crazy but . . ."

"But what?"

"But she don't say it in a crazy way."

"Not sure what you're getting at."

"Up home, I had this cousin on my mama's side, name of Billy. We called him Bible Billy. Always reading Scripture, praying, and fasting. Real Jesusy. Know the kind?"

"Oh yeah."

"A few years back, Billy took to what he called Proclaiming the Word. One week he'd make a fuss saying God didn't want us to eat meat. Says so in the Bible, he'd say. Next week, he started saying we oughta take up snakes in church. God wanted us to. Says so in the Bible, he'd say."

"Come on," I said. "He wasn't serious, was he?"

"Dead serious. And if you let him, he'd talk at you all day, maybe all night. He'd argue and preach, recite scriptures. If that didn't work--and it never did--he'd wave his big black Bible in your face and shout. Then next time you saw him he'd be talking up something completely different that God wanted. Says so in the Bible, he'd say."

"Yeah. But what's that got to do with the girl?"

"Well, like I said, what she says is crazy."

"No doubt about that. Just how the hell did she talk the Captain into sending her to Winslow?"

"Maybe cause she don't sound crazy."

"How can you not sound crazy when you're saying something crazy?"

Riley scratched his beard a little before answering. "Now Cousin Billy, he not only said crazy things, he always rambled on like somebody with a bad fever. Seemed he needed to change your mind so bad he just couldn't shut up."

"Like if you believed him that proved he was right."

"Maybe. But this girl ain't no Bible Billy. If you hadn't asked her, she wouldn't have said a thing about God and the Government and all."

"I suppose."

"Yes, Sir. She looked right at you and said it plain. Said like it was true, true whether you believed it or not. Said it like nothing was ever gonna change her mind."

"Yeah, but you don't believe her, do you?"

"Naw. Maybe she's just a different kind of crazy than old cousin Billy. Anyways, we don't have to figure it out. We just have to get her to Central Camp."

"Amen to that. I should get some sleep before my watch." I started to walk away.

I heard Riley's voice behind me. "Of course, maybe God did send her." Turning to him, all I could see was his shape in the darkness.

He said, "But I was hoping God'd do better by us than a girl in borrowed britches."

4

I was on watch at dawn. The girl was also awake, kneeling on her blanket, praying quietly. I waited until she was done to wake Riley.

We went back to the trail. It ran flat through woods, but about noon, it led out into a wide meadow, tall with grass. When we reached the middle of the meadow, we heard a distant humming noise. At first, I thought it was a swarm of bees, but it was the wrong pitch. Then I saw it in the eastern sky. As high up as a mountaintop, it looked like a big stiff-winged bird. I realized it was an airplane like in the old books.

My heart pounded as I listened to the humming get louder. I watched the airplane pass directly overhead. What would it be like to be up that high, I thought, to move that fast?

The airplane flew west and was soon out of sight over a ridge.

"What the hell was that?" Riley said.

"An airplane," I said.

"Be damn hard to hit that with a rifle."

"I saw this in the Spirit," the girl said. "The Government has many airplanes. They will shoot at us, or drop things that explode. Bombs."

Damn, I thought, how can we fight that? I had a weak squirmy feeling deep down inside. Fear.

Jane looked at us. She didn't seem frightened of the Government, its airplanes, or even of bombs. Maybe she didn't know any better.

"Let's go," she said.

Riley and I looked at one another. Neither of us liked being told what to do, especially by this strange girl. But it was time to go.

We moved into the woods and across small ridges and hills. About an hour before sunset, I was on point and the ground had flattened again. We continued until a dirt road cut across our path at a sharp angle. After a look up and down the road, I crossed and continued, following the trail.

I heard her call out, "We should go this way." Turning, I saw she was standing at the junction, pointing up the road. I walked back.

"Why?" I said. "Why the road?"

"I feel a leading of the Spirit," she said.

"I think the road curves around and meets the trail later," Riley said. "It'll add half a day, or more."

I turned to her. "The Captain said you were in a hurry."

"That's not important now," she said. "We should go where the Spirit leads."

"There will be houses," I said. "We might not find a place to camp. If we're on the road after dark, somebody might just set their dogs on us or start shooting."

"But with luck," Riley said, "somebody might feed us. Maybe get to sleep indoors."

"Sure, if we're lucky," I said. "But best to be safe."

"We best go where the Spirit leads," she said.

"The Captain told me to get you to Central as quick as I could," I said. "And that's what we're gonna do."

She turned and started up the road.

I wanted to grab her by the back of her coat and drag her up the damn trail. It was bad enough we had to go on this fool's errand without listening to her craziness. But when I looked at Riley, he shrugged. It didn't matter to him which way we went.

"Damn!" I said and hurried to catch up with her.

After about two miles, I saw a house ahead. I signaled for us to move slow and be quiet. We needed to be careful. But the girl kept walking toward the house. She slung her rifle over her shoulder, put her hands up in the air, and shouted, "Hey there! Hey!"

A big black dog ran from around the far corner of the house, barking. It got between the girl and the house. I put my rifle on the dog. If it charged her, I would have to kill it. Dogs at other houses up the road started barking too.

Jane called out, "Hey there! Hey! My name's Jane. Can you help us? Hey there!"

By now, the girl was only ten yards from the house, and the dog was still barking like crazy. I tried to keep it in my sights as it jumped and hopped about, baring its teeth and barking. Then something strange happened. The girl held her left arm out straight with the palm of her hand down. The dog stopped barking and looked at her. Then she lowered her arm real slow, and the dog sat down in the dirt. The other dogs, barking in the distance, kept at it, but this one sat panting, its tongue hanging out, calm and friendly.

I brought my rifle down and looked over at Riley. He shrugged.

The front door opened a crack and then wider. Someone inside spoke to the girl, and she answered, but I couldn't make out the words. She walked closer. More talk. Then she turned and called us to come in. Riley and I moved in slow. To my surprise, the dog didn't bark at us. An older man and woman were standing next to the girl. The woman was talking to her, smiling. The man, holding a pistol, was watching us, nervous. Then he smiled, put the pistol in his belt, and said, "Why, you're George Riley's boy!"

Riley smiled. "Yes Sir, I sure am. And you'd be Mr. Baker. Sorry, I didn't recognize you right off. How's your boy?" They shook hands and started talking.

The Bakers took us in and fed us. Riley and Mr. Baker caught up on family news, while Mrs. Baker and Jane talked as though they were old friends. I just ate, happy to have a home cooked meal. After dinner, we moved our chairs over by the fireplace to talk. As we settled down, I could see Mr. Baker looking curiously at the girl. I suppose he was about to ask why she was dressed like a man, traveling with Riley and me, and all that. And I was curious to see what would happen. But Mrs. Baker excused herself saying she had to look in on Sally, their granddaughter, in the back room. Jane went with her.

Mr. Baker explained that Sally's mother had taken ill last winter and died. Just a week ago, the little girl had fallen from a tree and hit her head. "Now she just lies there," he said, looking into the fire. "Reckon she's gonna die. When my boy comes home, his wife and daughter will both be gone."

After a long silence, Riley said, "Mr. Baker, you knew David Winslow, didn't you?"

I knew what Riley was doing. Old-timers like Mr. Baker loved to tell stories about David Winslow and the early days. It would take his mind off his troubles.

Mr. Baker brightened and said, "I not only knew Winslow, but I was there when it all began."

Riley and I knew the story. We had grown up hearing it. We could tell it.

"Now, I know you boys have heard about the Plague," Mr. Baker said, looking at us, "but if you didn't go through it yourself you just can't imagine how bad it was. God help me, I was scared. I pray you two boys will never be so scared."

That was how it was with old-timers. They always had to talk about the Plague. They had to tell you how bad it was even if they had told you before. It was as if they still couldn't believe it had happened, still couldn't believe they had come through it alive. Riley and I exchanged a glance. We would just have to let the old man talk it out.

Mr. Baker continued, no longer looking at us. "My wife and I got out of Waynesville and came up to the mountains, to a town where we both had kin. Winslow had a church there. While the rest of us was acting like scared rabbits, he saw decent people had no choice but to take care of themselves. When some looters raped and cut up a local girl, Winslow and some of us men in his congregation tracked them down, and brought them back."

"We blindfolded them," Mr. Baker said, still looking into the fire. "And Reverend Winslow had us take them out to a big tree right on the main road into town. We had plenty of rope, but none of us knew how to make a real hangman's noose, like we'd seen in movies. So we just used slipknots. We threw the ropes over a stout branch of that tree. Then we took off the blindfolds, and let those three bastards see what they was gonna get."

"Only three?" Riley said. "I'd heard there was five."

"I've heard five, but I've also heard four," I said.

"It was three," Mr. Baker said. "I was there. Twenty-six years in July. Remember it like yesterday."

Mrs. Baker and Jane came back in and took their seats by the fire. Mr. Baker didn't seem to notice them. The story was the only thing on his mind.

"Well, when those three saw the nooses, it was something. Two of them just pitched a fit, crying, saying they ain't done a thing, and all. But there was the one who had real backbone. He didn't so much as blink at the ropes. That sumbitch--"

Mrs. Baker interrupted, "Now Harold, I won't have that language in this house."

Mr. Baker looked like he was about to argue with her, but I guess he thought better of it and went back to the story. "Anyway, the first one set to cursing us and yelling about his 'constitutional rights.' Said he wanted a lawyer. Before the Plague that would've meant something, but it didn't anymore. Well, Winslow put the noose around his neck and gave him a chance to get right with God, ask forgiveness for his sins. And you know what that sum-- . . . that one did?"

I knew. But Mr. Baker wanted someone to ask. So I said, "What'd he do?"

"He spit at Winslow and cursed God. Can you imagine? He's raped and cut up an innocent girl and he's sure to burn for eternity, and he curses God, throws away a last chance at mercy. Can you imagine?"

Mr. Baker sat there shaking his head, still in wonder after all the years.

"Then we had to hang him. Winslow had us pull on the rope. Together we lifted him, and he died real slow, choking and kicking. You could feel it through the rope, jerking in your hands until he got still. Then we tied off the rope and let him hang there."

I looked at Jane. She was leaning forward, listening real close to Mr.

Baker. Nothing squeamish in her.

"I'm here to tell you," Mr. Baker continued, "that was something. I wasn't much more than a boy. Then to hang a man. With these hands." He held them up, fingers spread wide, and turned them over. He looked at them like they belonged to a stranger.

"And then you had to do it again," Jane said.

Mr. Baker looked at her, kind of surprised. For a moment, I thought he might forget the story and start talking to her.

But he said, "Yeah, and then we did it again." He looked back into the fire. "The next one prayed for mercy, all the mercy he could get. Maybe he thought we'd let him go, if he prayed. I didn't think he was sorry for what he'd done, not really. But that's for God to know. Not me."

He shook his head, "Anyway, when we hung that one, I thought my arms would give out. I almost let go. But I didn't cause nobody else did."

"And the last man?" Riley said. Like I told you, we all knew the story. But it was like in church. Everyone knows what comes next. You have to do it complete. If you don't finish, better not to start.

"The last man," Mr. Baker said, "didn't say or do much when it was his turn. Reckon he'd given up after seeing the other two die. Winslow put the rope around the man's neck, and we all got ready to haul him up. But then, Winslow stopped it and said to the man, 'I'm letting you go.' Well, of course, the man commenced crying and promising never to do anything bad again. But Winslow just hit him hard across the face and told him, 'Shut up. This is not mercy. You're my messenger. Go tell all the other filth. They come around here and they'll die too. You come back, I'll kill you myself.'"

Then Mr. Baker came to the part that always frightened me when I was a boy. I suppose the hangings didn't frighten me as much because I couldn't imagine what it was to strangle at the end of a rope. I had never seen it. Not back then. But I had seen accidents and blood. I had seen what sharp metal could do to flesh. So I could imagine what Winslow did next, and it scared me bad.

"So the man would never forget, and so he'd have to explain it to everyone he met," Mr. Baker said, "Winslow took a knife and cut a big X deep in the man's forehead."

"Like the mark God put on Cain," Mrs. Baker said.

"That's right," Mr. Baker continued. "Then Winslow let him go, and he ran down the road, blood pouring down his face. We all thought it was over and started to go, but Winslow called us back and preached us a sermon. Right there under those swaying bodies, he preached."

Mr. Baker turned to his wife. "Mother, where did you put my Bible? I want to read a scripture to them."

"Right where you left it," she said. "Behind you, on the table." While he was finding it, coming back, and flipping through the pages, she said, "Lose that head of his if it weren't attached."

"Here it is," he said, "Nehemiah, Chapter 4, Verse 14." He cleared his throat and read to us.

> And I looked, and rose up, and said unto the nobles, and to the rulers, and to the rest of the people, Be not ye afraid of them: remember the Lord, which is great and terrible, and fight for your brethren, your sons, and your daughters, your wives, and your houses.

He put down the Bible and said, "Now this was when the Jews had come back from exile in Babylon and Nehemiah was rebuilding the walls of Jerusalem against their enemies. Winslow said we was just like those Jews living in the ruins. We had to build a wall against our enemies too. He told us to remember the Lord and to fight. He said the bodies would hang there as a warning to others and a reminder to us."

"And they hung there," Mrs. Baker said, "until they rotted right off the ropes. It was a terrible thing, like to make you sick, but we sure never forgot."

"That was the beginning," Mr. Baker said. "The militia, thinking of ourselves as a people, all the things David Winslow did for us. And I was there."

"So was I," Mrs. Baker said.

I had heard the story many times. When I was seven, I memorized that verse from Nehemiah to recite in front of my church. But I had never heard the story from folks who were there.

"Mr. Baker," I said. "I always wanted to know. Why did Reverend Winslow have everyone pull on those ropes by hand? I mean, I saw a hanging once, and that wasn't the way it was done."

Mr. Baker nodded and said, "Winslow told us we had to do it with our own hands, and we had to do it together. And . . ." Then he stopped talking, his lower lip trembling. He was staring behind us.

We all turned and saw a little girl shuffling across the floor to Mrs. Baker. "Nana, I'm hungry," said the little girl.

Mrs. Baker fell to her knees and wrapped the child in a tight embrace. Weeping, she kissed the child.

Mr. Baker stumbled over to them and knelt down. "How?" he said. "How'd this happen? How?"

"It was her," Mrs. Baker said, pointing at Jane. "She prayed. She laid hands on Sally. Asked God's blessing. Healed her."

I looked at Jane. She was leaning forward, eyes closed tight, whispering. Praying.

After a moment, Mrs. Baker turned and embraced Jane. "Thank you. Thank you. You healed her," she said.

Jane let the woman embrace her for a bit and then she stood up. She put her right hand on the old woman's gray head and said, "Only God can heal. Give the praise to God."

Then Jane said, "Sally's hungry. We best feed her." She led the weeping old couple and the confused child over to the kitchen.

It took a while for all the excitement to die down. Until it did, I sat there and avoided looking at Riley. Finally, Mr. Baker took Riley and me out to a shed to sleep. Jane would stay in the house.

After we had laid out our blankets, we sat and listened to the night.

"So," Riley said, "whatcha think?"

"I think Mr. Baker tells a good story."

"Come on. What about Jane?"

"We just happened to be here when that little girl woke up. She just got well. Luck. Coincidence. That's all."

Riley snorted and said, "Just happened? Just happened to be here? Jane just happened to pick this road. And then the little girl just happened to wake up."

"OK. Go ahead and believe Jane healed that little girl. But you just remember she also says God told her to go to war, to save our people from the Government."

"Well, when you put it that way, it sounds crazy."

"Damn right."

"You believe the stories in the Bible, like all the miracles, are true?"

"Yes, of course," I said. "What's that got to do with anything?"

"Well, it seems to me some of those stories might sound crazy . . . if you didn't believe in the Bible. Which, of course, you do."

"Riley, those things happened in the Holy Land thousands of years ago. This is here. This is now."

"True enough, but God's still everywhere, ain't He? And we could sure use some miracles right here and right now."

Damn, I thought, he had me.

Riley continued, "Maybe Jane can do miracles. Maybe she can't. I reckon we oughta wait and see."

After that, Riley went to sleep. I lay awake in the dark determined not to believe, yet wanting to believe.

5

In the morning, we had a hard time getting away from the Bakers. They fed us a big breakfast, but Riley and I could have walked out in the middle of the meal. I doubt the Bakers would have noticed. They just didn't want Jane to leave. They wanted to keep thanking her. Jane was nice enough about it, but she just kept saying, "We have to go."

When we left, the Bakers were standing in front of the house, tears on their cheeks. The little girl stood to one side watching all this, not crying, but just looking at Jane as though she were trying hard to figure out something. Jane gave them one last wave from the road as we headed out. Then she turned to me and said, "We have to hurry."

This made me mad. She had taken this longer road. I almost said something, but if she wanted to hurry, I would be done with her that much sooner. Good riddance.

We walked up the road all day, occasionally passing a house. Nobody paid much attention to us, but the dogs would bark at us until long after we went out of sight.

Around noon, we sat down for a rest and had some food and water. Jane didn't want to stop. "We have to hurry," she said again.

I turned away, letting Riley explain.

"We ain't gonna get there before dark, no matter," he said. "We'll have to camp."

I looked back to see her reaction. She seemed to start to say something and then stopped. Sitting on a rock, she took out her water and drank. Riley offered her some of the food the Bakers had given us, but she refused.

Riley and I were quiet while we ate and drank. I wanted to sleep. I had dreamt of the blue-eyed man the night before. It was always worse when I woke up in some strange place, and harder to get back to sleep.

When he had finished eating, Riley said, "Hey Jane, how'd you do that with the dog?"

"Dog?" she said.

"You know. The Baker's dog was barking like crazy, and you just settled him down." He extended his arm with the palm down and lowered it just the way she had.

"Oh that. Don't know. Just did it." Then she put away her water and stood up, ready to go.

Late in the day, we got back to the trail. Just before sunset, Riley and I picked out a campsite and started gathering wood and settling in. Jane wanted to push on even if we arrived after dark.

"We ain't gonna do that," I said. I didn't bother to keep the anger out of my voice.

"Why not?" she said. She was still standing on the trail, still wanting to keep going.

"The boys on guard duty get a mite jumpy after dark," he said. "Apt to shoot at anything that moves. So no need to hurry up there and maybe get shot. Best wait 'til morning. Come on, we need some wood."

She looked up the trail. For a moment, I thought she might head off on her own again. But she didn't. Leaning her rifle against a tree, she started gathering wood.

We had a big fire and ate the rest of the food the Bakers had given us. Jane just sat, staring into the fire.

Two hours after full dark, we heard the patrol coming. The first sound, a cracked twig, startled Jane, and she reached for her rifle.

"Be still," I said.

Riley called out, "You boys from Central?"

A voice came out of the darkness, "Yeah. Who're you?"

"Three of us," Riley said. "We're militia."

I heard whispering out in the darkness, but I couldn't make out the words.

"Take it easy," the voice said. "Coming in."

"Come on then," Riley said.

Four figures came out of the dark toward us. I could just make out their faces when one of them said, "Hey Riley."

"That you Frye?" Riley said.

"Sure is. You doing okay?"

"Tolerable. You?"

All four men squatted by the fire. Frye grinned at us, but the others didn't look friendly. One man, older than the rest, said, "What's your business here?"

I pulled out the written orders the Captain had given me. The man was looking them over when Frye said, "I'll be goddamned. A girl."

Jane said, "Don't curse."

The other three looked up and peered at Jane in surprise. The older man said to her, "What you doing here, girl?"

She said, "My name is--"

I interrupted. "Like it says, she's going to Central Camp. The reason ain't your concern." I didn't want her to start talking about God and all her nonsense.

The older man handed the paper back and said, "Frye, take them up to camp. They can sort it out."

It took an hour or more for Frye to get us up to the camp and through the front gate. Somebody else took us over to a shed to see the officer on duty, a Lieutenant Gordon. He sat behind a table and looked sleepy and annoyed. Unlike Riley and me, Gordon's clothes and boots were clean. There was no dirt under his fingernails, and his beard was neatly trimmed.

This one, I thought, doesn't go on patrols.

The three of us stood before the table. I gave him the orders and the sealed letter. He only glanced at the orders. But as he went through the letter, he smiled like something was very funny.

"So, little lady," he said to Jane, "you talk to God."

"I must see Charles Winslow," she said.

"General Winslow is a busy man," Gordon said. Riley and I exchanged a glance. We had never heard Winslow called "General" before. His father had never bothered with titles.

"I must see Winslow," she said. "What I have to say cannot wait."

Gordon no longer looked amused. "Come back tomorrow," he said, "and we'll see what we can do." He called to a man outside the door and told him to show us where we could camp.

Jane stomped out and Riley followed. But I stayed to tell Gordon about the airplane. When, where, and all that. He said they had seen the airplane too and told me to go.

"Sir," I said. "We had to bring this girl here. Can we go back to our unit in the morning?"

"I see why you want to be done with this . . . this business. But no. If you go, someone else will have to watch her and then take her back where she belongs. So I need you to stay with her. She won't be here long."

"Yes, Sir," I said.

When I caught up to Riley, he said, "What kept you?"

"Told him about the airplane . . . and I asked if we could go home. He said we have to stay with her."

"Good," Riley said, "I want to be around if Jane shoots that peckerwood Lieutenant."

In the morning, Jane went back to see Lieutenant Gordon. A man outside the shed told her Gordon was busy and couldn't see her now. He said she should come back later, maybe tomorrow. Instead of going away, Jane sat outside the shed, beneath a nearby tree. Riley joined her. I decided to take look around the camp. It was built on a hill and protected by a ten-foot high palisade. The lower part of the camp, where we had slept the night before, was like all the other militia camps: Lean-tos, ratty tents, sheds, cooking fires, and men like Riley and me in rough beards and dirty clothes.

Up the hill, things were different. There were log and plank cabins. Like Lieutenant Gordon, everyone up there had better clothes and boots, and they trimmed their beards. Winslow's house was at the top. It was a two-level brick building with a porch and a big front entrance. I was surprised to see the house was ringed with barbed wire and had guards all around it.

I stood just beyond the barbed wire, and I noticed the guards were watching me real close. Maybe it was because they hadn't seen me around camp before, or maybe because I was so dirty. A Lieutenant came over and stood in front of me on the other side of the wire. He said, "What's your business here?"

"No business, Sir. I'd just never seen this before." I gestured toward the house. I wanted to ask about all the barbed wire, but I thought better of it.

"You've seen it now. Move along."

The way he said it made me angry, angry enough to fight. But he was an officer, and I would have to climb through barbed wire just to get to him. So I said, "Yes, Sir," and started down the hill. After a few steps, I looked over my shoulder and saw he was still standing at the wire, watching me. I went down the hill slow, trying not to let anger get the best of me.

Jane and Riley were still sitting where I had left them.

When I walked up, Riley said, "Hey."

"Hey," I said and noticed Jane didn't even look at me. She was watching for Gordon.

"Have a good look around?"

"Yeah."

"Well, maybe I'll take a look too. You gonna be here?" As he said, "here," he tilted his head toward Jane, who still seemed to be ignoring us.

I just shrugged and sat down.

As Riley walked away, I said, "Watch you don't get too close to Winslow's house."

He stopped and gave me a puzzled look.

I felt like telling about how that Lieutenant had treated me like dirt. But I just said, "Ain't very friendly up there. You'll see what I mean."

Riley nodded and walked away. I turned toward Jane and was surprised to see her looking at me. After a moment, she turned back to watch Gordon's shed.

Jane remained silent and so did I. There was nothing to do but watch the men coming and going from the shed. Some glanced her way and, for a moment, saw nothing but a boy wearing his daddy's big coat. Then they would look back, amazed to see a girl. Walking away, they would whisper to one another and look over their shoulders at her. One man was so busy staring, he tripped on a tree root and fell down. The men with him laughed like it was the funniest damn thing ever seen. If Jane took notice of the stares or the foolishness, she gave no sign. She sat silent and still, like a hunter waiting for game.

Watching all this, I began to feel bad for her. She was all alone, without kin or friend, the only girl in the whole camp. Of course, she had aggravated me some, and I did think she was crazy. But I had seen no weakness or complaint in her. And she seemed to mean every damn word she said, even if she was talking nonsense.

It was about noon when Gordon came out of the shed. Jane stiffened, getting ready to be called over, getting ready to go meet Charles Winslow. Gordon, however, didn't look toward Jane. He yawned and stretched before pulling a pipe and tobacco pouch from a pocket. He carefully loaded the pipe and sent a guard to fetch a brand from a nearby cooking fire. Gordon lit his pipe with it, took a few good puffs, and exhaled looking up at the clouds. Only then, did he glance at Jane. Then he turned to the man who had fetched the brand for him. Gordon said something to him. They both laughed. Then Gordon went back in the shed.

Gordon hadn't been laughing at me, but he reminded me of the other Lieutenant up the hill and the way I'd been treated. That made me mad. Before I hadn't cared, but now I hoped she would get to see Winslow. She was crazy, but I wanted her to have that much. Then Jane turned to me and she nodded, nodded the way she had when I first saw her.

Aside from going off to fetch some food for us, I spent the rest of the day sitting there with Jane, watching the comings and goings in silence. We didn't see Gordon again, and nobody spoke to us. Riley never came back.

At sunset, Jane and I went to where we had camped. Riley was there, just finishing building a lean-to for Jane. He even had an old blanket to hang over the opening.

"It won't keep out much rain," he said, "but I reckon you could use a little privacy."

"Much obliged," she said and sat down. Riley and I got a fire going, and we ate a little. After a while, Riley wandered away to see if he could find a friend he had run into earlier in the day.

Jane just sat looking into the fire. And I looked at Jane.

I reckoned she was about 17, the age when most of our young women got married. Given what she was doing, I doubted Jane was promised to anyone. Despite her chopped up hair, Jane had a pleasant enough face, but she wasn't what you would call pretty. Under all the men's clothes, she probably had a sturdy frame, and from what I could tell, her teeth were good. My mother always said that was a sign of good health. I wondered what she would look like if she dressed like other girls.

When I found myself thinking this, I felt guilty. Jesus said, "Whosoever looketh on a woman to lust after her hath committed adultery with her in his heart." I was promised to Maggie, even though she was pretty much a stranger. So I ought not to be thinking about any other girl, and especially not one who believed God told her things. I was still looking at her when she glanced up. I turned away. To hide my embarrassment, I asked her where she was from.

She told me she was from a little town with just a few families. Her father and mother had four acres and they raised chickens and some pigs. She had an older sister, who had just been married, and a younger brother "who can hardly wait," she said with a laugh, "to be in the militia." I laughed too, remembering how impatient I had been to leave home when I was younger.

I wanted to ask if she was promised to anyone up home, but I thought better of it. Instead, I asked about the old man who had come with her to the first camp.

"That's my Uncle John. My parents didn't believe in my mission. Uncle John did. He helped me convince that captain to send me here. Uncle John wanted to come, but he couldn't. He just couldn't bear all the walking. And besides, he's a preacher with a congregation."

"What kind of preacher?"

"Church of God. We believe in all the gifts of the Holy Spirit. You know what that means?"

"Sure. I've known Church of God people."

"Now, we don't hold with handling snakes, drinking poison, or any of that 'signs' foolishness."

I nodded, but I was thinking, Handling snakes might be safer than what you're trying to do.

"What about you?" she said, smiling. "I take you for a pretty starchy Baptist."

I laughed and told her she was right. My family had been Baptists of one sort or another for generations. Then I started talking about my family and our farm, though I didn't mention Maggie. And for a while, we were just two people passing the time. Then I asked about her messages from God. I just couldn't help but be curious.

"Do you want to know? For real?"

"Tell me."

She drew a long breath as if gathering her strength. "Sometimes the message is a feeling that blows through me. It's like a strong wind in the trees. Everything in me just bends to it. Sometimes, it's words, just a few simple words. I hear them inside, but it's not like thinking. It's not like a voice. The words are just there."

I said nothing.

"Sometimes, I pray, and God puts a picture in my heart. At first, I may not know what it means. But if I keep holding it in my heart, I understand. Sometimes it's a dream. I knew when David Winslow died. God gave a dream. Clear as anything. I didn't tell anyone about it, but when we heard he'd died, I knew God had a purpose for me."

I still said nothing.

"Ever since, God has been showing me through the Spirit the dangers our people face. And He has showed me what I must do."

"You really think Winslow will talk with you?"

"If it's God's will, it will happen. And it is God's will."

"But that Lieutenant Gordon won't give you the time of day. How are you going to get to Winslow?"

"Don't know. If God wants it, He will make a way. I just have to be ready."

"And God wants this war? I mean, He wants us to fight the Government?"

Jane looked at me and said. "You've killed?"

"Yeah," I said. Her look made me feel uncomfortable. And I remembered the feel of the blue-eyed man's throat in my hands.

"Why?"

"They were thieves and raiders. It was my duty."

"I'm glad you did your duty. But if you can kill for an earthly reason, why not kill for a heavenly reason, for God?"

Riley stumbled into the light of our fire and sat down. From the smell of him, I guessed he and his friend had shared some homebrewed whiskey.

When I turned back to Jane, she was already behind the blanket in her lean-to.

Soon Riley lay down, and I helped him get under his blankets. Before long, he was snoring softly as he always did. He never had trouble going to sleep. A little whiskey only made it easier. I built up our fire a little and got under my blanket. I didn't go to sleep right away. Instead, I watched the fire burn and thought about what Jane had said, "Why not kill for God?"

Jane, I thought, what if you're wrong about what God wants?

And then I thought, What if she's right?

6

I slammed the blue-eyed man's head against the rock. He was trying to rip my hands from his throat. But then his hands turned weak and fell away. I could barely breathe from the effort as I hit his head on the rock. Then I heard that wet cracking sound.

I opened my eyes and saw the sky. Dawn. I sat up, breathing hard, shaking. Then I realized Jane was sitting outside her lean-to, watching me. I didn't want her to see me like this.

She said something, but I didn't understand.

"What?" I said.

"A dream?"

"Yeah."

"Bad?"

"Yeah, bad."

I had the feeling she wanted me to tell her about the dream. Some folks say it helps to talk, but I wouldn't do it. Just couldn't. Especially not with her. I got up, grabbed my rifle, and walked away.

I wanted to keep clear of Jane, of everybody, for a while. As soon as the sun got up, she would go to Gordon again and demand to see Charles Winslow. Riley would go with her. They didn't need me. So I wandered around the camp. I thought some about things Jane had said last night, but mostly I just wanted to be alone.

All that stopped when a man stepped in front of me. He was filthy, and his nose was large and misshapen, like it had been broken a few times. "Hey," he said, "ain't you one of them what brought in that girl?"

Every camp, like every little town, has its bully. I was just today's sport for this one. But I wouldn't play.

"You're crowding me," I said.

"How come she's wearing britches and all?" the man said. "Something wrong with her?"

"None of your concern."

"What's she doing here?"

"Out of my way." I said each word slow.

He stepped aside and let me pass. Then he said, "Hey, how much she charge for a quick fuck?"

I turned and hit him with the stock of my rifle. He landed on the ground with blood all over his right ear. I was about to start working him over with my boots when the some of the other men around grabbed me and pulled me back. I lost my rifle and hat as I struggled. By the time, the man I had hit was back on his feet, a big man was between us, shouting, "Stop it!"

Everyone around me stopped, but I was still trying to get loose. The big man put one hand on my chest and looked me in the eye. He said, "You want to fight me, boy?"

I looked up at him. He was half a head taller than me and wore the insignia of a squad leader. I shook my head and stood still.

He looked at me a moment longer and said, "Let him go." The men were slow to obey, and I wrenched my arms free. After straightening my coat, I picked up my hat and rifle, and set off as slow as I could. I didn't look back as I went down the hill.

When I got to Jane and Riley, still waiting for Gordon, both looked at me.

"Hey," Riley said.

"Hey," I said.

"Where you been?"

"Round about."

"Anything wrong?"

I just shook my head. I would tell him later. Jane looked at me a moment longer and then turned back to watch for Gordon. I sat. It would take me a while to settle down. I had been in enough fights to know once you got your blood up it was hard to stop, and harder to get over it. The thing that bothered me most is why I even hit that man. I made him move aside. Then I hit him because he'd said something about Jane. I'd given him a way to get under my skin.

I was thinking about my stupidity when a man walked up and said to Jane, "There's some folks here for you. Down at the east gate."

"For me? What folks?" Jane said.

"Don't know. They just ask for, 'the girl who heals.' That make any sense to you?"

Jane said she would come.

We went out through the front gate to a field at the eastern side the camp. Maybe a dozen people stood, waiting. When they saw Jane coming, they rushed forward, surrounding her, all talking at once.

Riley and I looked at each other and shrugged. We asked one man at the edge of the crowd why he was here. He said he had heard Jane had healed a little girl.

Riley said, "This is getting right interesting."

"Look," I said and nodded toward the far side of the field, where the trail came out of the woods. A woman, almost staggering, carried a child on her back. Just behind her, two men bore a skinny little boy on a pallet. A woman walked next to the boy, talking to him, pointing across the field to Jane.

"Damn, more of 'em," Riley said. "What do we do now?"

I shrugged and said, "Don't know."

But Jane knew. She handed her rifle to me and led everyone over to one edge of the field where the people could rest in the shade. Growing up, I had seen a fair number of traveling preachers and even a few who claimed to do healings. All of them put on a big show of standing up and, well, preaching at folks. I had always treated such preachers as free entertainment.

Maybe I should have known better by then, but I expected Jane to put on a show, to start preaching about her messages from God and all that. But she didn't. Instead, she just had a little private time with folks. Sometimes it was a whole family carrying a sick child, or one of their old folks, to see Jane. Sometimes it was just a mother or a father with a baby. She just visited with them, listened to each and every one of them. She would pray and lay hands upon the sick and the hurt. You could hear other folks praying along with her. A few had their arms lifted up and were speaking in tongues. Other folks who had been with Jane, or were still waiting, took to singing the old hymns everyone knew.

Riley and I stayed busy helping newcomers get settled. And they kept coming. Soon we had fifty people in the crowd. Men from the camp were drifting down to watch the strange doings. After two hours or so, I saw Lieutenant Gordon and another officer, a thin gray-haired man, coming toward us.

Gordon waved me over. "What's going on here?" He sounded angry.

I explained about the healing at the Baker place, and I guessed that the story had spread.

"Why didn't you tell me about this?"

"Didn't seem important, Sir. We didn't know these people would come here."

"They have to go. Move them. Now."

"No, Lieutenant," the other officer said. "We don't treat our people like livestock." He called to one of the men on guard duty, "Bring down some food and water for these folks. Whatever you can find. Anyone gives you trouble, tell them Colonel Campbell sent you." He said to Gordon, "You can go. I'll see to this."

Gordon looked angry, but he said, "Yes, Sir."

I watched him walk away. Good riddance, I thought.

The Colonel took a step toward me and said, "Tell me about the girl."

I told him what Jane had said about her mission from God, fighting the Government, what had happened at the Baker place, how Gordon had treated her, everything. He listened and looked at the crowd around Jane. From his questions, I could tell he already knew some things, likely from the sealed letter I had brought. But he wanted to hear it all from me.

When I was done, he said, "You believe her?"

"Sir, I don't know what to believe. But she believes."

"That might be enough. I'd like to talk with her."

I led him down to Jane, who stood up when she saw him coming, and shook hands with him as any man would have done. They walked off a little way together. I watched as they spoke, but couldn't hear what was said. Each looked directly at the other. Neither smiled, but each nodded as the other spoke. He gave a final nod and walked away.

He came to me and said, "If she needs anything, let me know. I'm Colonel Campbell, General Winslow's Chief of Staff."

"Yes, Sir," I said, and I watched him head back into camp.

Riley came up. "What happened?"

"Not sure," I said, "but I think Jane just found her first friend up on the hill."

"About damn time," he said.

People kept arriving in twos and threes all through the afternoon. When Jane left them, perhaps seventy people were camped for the night in the field. As we walked to our campsite, I could tell she was worn out. So I didn't bother to ask what Campbell had said to her. She went right into her lean-to without saying goodnight.

Riley and I got a fire going and talked quietly so as not to disturb Jane.

"So," Riley said, "whatcha think?"

"Don't know."

"Still think she's crazy?"

"Don't know."

"Don't know? After what we saw today? You still don't know?"

"That's right. I still don't know. Yeah, she took good care of these folks, but it's got nothing to do with a war with the Government, now does it?"

"Come on. If Jane hadn't healed that little girl, none of them would be here. We'd still be waiting on that Lieutenant Gordon."

"So you reckon she can do miracles?" I said.

"Yes, I reckon she can."

"You ain't gone Jesusy on me, have you?"

"No, I ain't gone Jesusy. But partner, comes a time when you shit or get off the pot."

I felt pulled toward what Riley wanted me to say, but something in me just wouldn't do it. I said, "Well, I don't know."

He stood up, snatched his rifle, and walked off into the darkness. After a while, I got my bedroll and lay down for the night. But, of course, I didn't go to sleep for a long time. I lay thinking, fighting the things Riley had said.

The dream of the blue-eyed man started the way it always did. We fought until I had him down. While he struggled to get free, I tried to slam his head against the rock. And then everything changed. The blue-eye man looked up at me and spoke, even though my hands squeezed his throat. He said, "Let me go." His voice was calm.

"No!" I said.

"Let me go."

"No!" I tried to slam his head against the rock. But I couldn't move him. I felt weak.

"Let me go."

I cried out, terrified of what he would do to me. Yet part of was glad to be done, glad to die. Maybe there would be some peace in it. So I let go of his throat, ready to take whatever came next.

Then I was awake, lying in the twisted blankets of my bedroll. It was dawn.

I jumped a little when Jane spoke, just a few feet away.

"He's gone," she said.

She couldn't know about the blue-eyed man. I had never told anyone. But somehow, she did. I turned and looked at her, squatting next to the ashes of our fire, holding her rifle with both hands. My mouth was very dry.

"You let him go," she said.

"What's it mean?" My voice was shaky.

I wanted to know what she was going to say. But I also wanted to run from her, from my bad dreams, from the militia, from my family and Maggie, from the future itself. Yet she held me.

"It means you're free," she said. "If you want to be." She stood up and walked away, disappearing into the trees. Shivering, I sat up and watched her go. Then I wiped my tears away with the sleeve of my coat.

That morning, when Jane got to the field in front of the camp, at least a hundred people were waiting for her, with more arriving all day. Riley and I worked as before, settling the newcomers and making sure the water and food kept coming. Several times, I saw Campbell watching from a distance, but he didn't come down to speak to Jane.

She listened to folks and prayed, laid hands upon the sick and suffering, but there were no sudden healings, no miracles. If those folks were disappointed, I didn't see it. They prayed and sang, shared the food and water, and watched Jane with eyes full of hope.

During a quiet stretch in the afternoon, when no new folks had shown up for a while, I found Riley standing back from the crowd. I walked over slow and stood next to him. For a little time, we were quiet, just watching Jane. It was up to me to speak first, and I knew it.

"Thought about what you were saying last night."

"Yeah."

"About shitting or getting off the pot."

"I recall."

"Well . . . I'm shitting."

Riley laughed. "Damn, but don't you just have a way with words. Must be all that education you got."

Grinning, I didn't say anything. Riley was quiet too. We stood there for a while watching Jane and the crowd. It was nice, this feeling of being in this together--whatever this was.

It was close to sunset when we were finished for the day. Jane was working her way through the crowd toward the camp, when a man walked up with a folded piece of paper. He handed it to me and said, "It's for the girl. Urgent."

I took the message to Jane.

She was at the edge of the crowd when I reached her. She took the paper, unfolded it, and looked at it for a long moment.

"I can't read," she said.

I took it and read aloud. "General Winslow wishes to meet you. Please come to his residence as soon as possible."

She took the message from me and looked at it again. She whispered a few words I couldn't hear. Then she turned back to the crowd and held the paper up in the air. "Let us praise God for the mountains He moves when we have faith," she shouted. "Charles Winslow, the leader of our people, will meet with me. I'm sorry. I'll not be with you again, for now God has other work for me. Go home and tell everyone that a new day has dawned. Please keep me, our people, and our leader in your prayers. In God's name, we will prevail."

The crowd burst with excited talk and shouts. Those closest to Jane hugged her. Others hugged whoever was standing close by. I heard snatches of shouted prayers. It was that time of day, when for a few moments, the light of the setting sun becomes golden. I looked at the joyful faces, the faces that had made the important men on the hill pay attention to this unimportant girl. The moment was golden.

I looked for Riley and saw him standing apart. He didn't look happy. I went over to him.

"Good news," I said.

"Great news," he said.

"So why don't you look like it's great?"

He squinted and scratched his beard. "Can't help thinking of something my mama used to say."

"What's that?"

"'Be careful what you wish for, cause you might get it.'"

I turned back to the crowd. The golden light had faded.

7

Everyone in camp knew we were going to see Winslow. Silent and curious, they lined the path and stared at Jane as she walked up the hill. Riley and I followed along a step or two behind.

Campbell was waiting at the entrance to the building and greeted her. Then he told Riley and me, "You'll wait here."

Jane pointed at me and said, "No. He has to come."

I'm not sure who was more surprised, Campbell or me.

"Why?" Campbell said.

"He has to come," she said.

Campbell paused and seemed to make some sort of calculation. He said, "All right, Jane."

After Jane and I handed our rifles to the guards, Campbell took us inside. We went through an anteroom and down a hallway to a set of double doors. As we went in, Campbell turned to me and pointed to a spot just to the left of the doorway. I understood he wanted me to stand there and say nothing, do nothing. That was fine with me. I had no business being there.

The room was square and had a nice rug on the floor. There were maps hanging on the walls and shelves filled with books. The room made me think of how dirty I was and how bad I smelled. In the corner nearest me, a Lieutenant sat at a small writing desk. Campbell turned and started speaking with him. On the other side of the room, six men were standing, talking to one another. One man was taller than the others, thick through the middle, and balding. His back was to the door, and as we came in, he let out a booming laugh that filled the room. I guessed he must be Charles Winslow.

In the time it took me to take all this in, Jane had crossed the room and come up behind a short man standing with the others. I couldn't see his face and didn't know who he was. Jane put a hand on his shoulder. When he turned around and Jane put a hand over her heart and said loudly, "Charles Winslow, I am Jane Darcy. I have a message from the Lord. He will protect our people and drive out the enemy. Let me fight and He will give us victory."

Jane bowed her head and went to her knees, praying. Everyone was still. After a long moment, the short man said to her, "Um . . . please, please stand up. Please." He sounded embarrassed, unsure of himself. Jane stood up, and I realized I had been holding my breath.

"How did you know who I was?" he said to her. It was a good question. He was clean-shaven and had a fat little belly. He didn't resemble his father, who had been tall and hard-looking with a long full beard. Charles Winslow was the softest-looking man in the room.

"The Spirit led me to you," Jane said. Then she turned to the rest of us. "We must speak alone. Leave us." It was a command.

No one moved. Everyone was waiting to see what Winslow would do. After a long moment, he nodded. The men moved slowly toward the door, glancing back at Jane and Winslow. I was the last out, shutting it behind me.

Outside, I stood next to the door, trying my best to be invisible. Campbell and his Lieutenant, both looking miserable, stood together in the hallway. The other men waited in the anteroom. The tall man looked very angry. His arms were across his chest, and his face was red. He wasn't an officer, but I had the feeling he was used to giving orders.

A minute passed. Then five. The tall man paced around the anteroom and up and down the hallway. The other men made way for him.

He had passed me a few times when he stopped in front of me, and looked me up and down. He turned to Campbell and said, "Just who the hell is he?"

"He brought the girl here," Campbell said. "She insisted he come with her."

"Insisted?! Insisted?!" the tall man said. "Who is she to insist on anything?" He stared hard at Campbell. But Campbell stared back. Just as hard.

The tall man started pacing again. Another five minutes. Then ten.

I wondered why I was there. Why had she wanted me here? What was I supposed to be doing?

The door opened. Jane and Winslow came out. Winslow was smiling. He appeared happy as he touched Jane's shoulder and said to Campbell, "Please make sure this remarkable young woman is taken care of." Campbell told his Lieutenant to see to it.

Winslow turned to Jane. "We'll speak again soon."

Jane nodded slowly.

Then Winslow said, "Gentlemen," and gestured for the others to come back into the room. Jane stepped aside and stood watching until the door closed.

We went out, got our rifles back, and found Riley. Campbell's Lieutenant had someone take us to a cabin. We went in and discovered Jane had a bed with real sheets, and a table and chairs for meals. Riley and I went back to our campsite for our bedrolls and the makings of Jane's lean-to. Just as we returned, two men showed up with some hot food for us.

When the men had cleared out, and it was just the three of us again, Riley let out a low whistle and started dishing out big plates of food.

Over dinner, I told Riley how Jane had just walked in and taken over. Jane smiled as I told the story. I also told what went on in the hallway and had them both laughing with an imitation of the tall man asking, "Just who the hell is he?"

Then I asked Jane, "Why'd you want me in there? It's not like I could help."

"I wanted someone on my side," she said.

"Ain't Campbell on your side?" Riley said.

Jane shook her head.

Riley and I exchanged a look. I turned back to Jane and said, "Well, why me? Why not Riley?"

She shrugged. "The Spirit chose you."

Riley and I exchanged another look. That was all the answer we were going to get. We were quiet for a bit.

"Jane, what did you and Winslow say?" I said.

She smiled, stood up, and said good night.

Riley and I went out, put out our bedrolls, and built a fire. We sat for a long time warming ourselves without talking. Finally, I said, "Leaves a lot unsaid, don't she?"

"That she does."

"Wonder why."

"Maybe God don't explain. Just tells her what to do."

"Maybe," I said, even though I suspected there was more to it than that.

We sat for a while and then Riley said he was going to turn in. Soon, I could hear him snoring. I sat at the fire and thought about all that had happened since morning. I thought about my dream with the blue-eyed man. It was strange, but I knew, knew for a fact, I would not dream of him again, at least not the way I used to. That felt good.

And I thought about how Jane would not tell us what she and Winslow had said. I realized then she would never tell. By tomorrow everyone in camp, and in a week or two all of our people, would know she had spoken with Winslow alone, but no one would know what they had said.

The secret is power, I thought. It makes her Winslow's equal.

8

In the morning, Jane got word Winslow wanted to talk to her again. Campbell's Lieutenant brought us to the same room as the night before.

Campbell, the tall man, and another man I hadn't seen before, sat at a table in the center of the room. Winslow sat at the head of the table, but the smile of the night before was gone. Instead, he looked nervous and glanced back and forth between Campbell and the tall man.

Jane took the empty seat. I stood to the left of the door.

The tall man cleared his throat and thanked Jane for coming. He said he was David Jackson, Chairman of General Winslow's Council of Advisors, and the other man was Reverend William Maxwell. "And, of course, you know General Winslow and Colonel Campbell."

Jackson wasn't angry anymore. He looked like a cat about to jump on a mouse.

"We wanted to talk with you," Jackson continued, "to ask a few questions about you and the . . . the claims that you've been making. Would that be all right?"

Jane said nothing. A nod.

"Perhaps you could tell us about yourself, your family, your upbringing?" Reverend Maxwell said.

Jane told them about her family and her farm. She said she was about 17 years old, and all she had ever done was clean, cook, sew, and work on the farm. Until this journey, she had never been more than a few miles from home. I couldn't see Jane's face, but her voice was calm and even.

"Do you know how to read and write?" Jackson said.

"No. Don't know A from B," she said.

Maxwell smiled and said, "Is Jesus Christ your personal Lord and Savior?"

42

"Yes," Jane said.

"And you believe the Bible is the Word of God?"

"Yes."

"And you keep the Commandments?"

"Yes."

Jackson said, "But you dress in men's clothes?"

"Yes," Jane said.

Jackson smiled and reached for a Bible that lay open on the table. "Well, the Bible says in Deuteronomy, Chapter 22, verse 5." He paused and cleared his throat before reading, "The woman shall not wear that which pertaineth unto a man, neither shall a man put on a woman's garment: for all that do so are abomination unto the LORD thy God."

He put the Bible down and smiled. The cat had pounced.

Jane said, "God didn't call me to be a man, but to go to war. So I dress for fighting."

"But the Bible calls it 'abomination.'"

"Jesus said to the Pharisees, you 'strain at a gnat and swallow a camel.' My britches don't matter. What matters is what God wants us to do about the Government's army. Let's talk about that."

Jackson didn't answer, but his face was getting red again. Winslow and Campbell sat silent, watching. Maxwell, looking uncomfortable, cleared his throat and said, "You say God has given you messages?"

"Yes," she said.

"And God has given you a mission?"

"Yes."

"Now, please don't take offense, but I think we've all heard of folks who claim God spoke to them. Then they've gone out and done some terrible things. Wicked things."

"Yes, that's true."

"I'd say those folks were listening to the Devil, not God."

"Yes, I agree."

"So how do you know that your mission is from God rather than Devil?"

"God sent me to save our people from our enemies. And that's what this militia's for. You ever asked if this militia is doing God's work or the Devil's? Of course not. Foolish question."

Maxwell opened his mouth to speak, but nothing came out. I reckon he wasn't used to 17-year-old girls calling him a fool.

Then I noticed that Jackson was looking hard at the minister, disgusted. He turned to Jane. "You claim to have healed a little girl?"

"Only God can heal," Jane said. "I prayed with Mrs. Baker for the child. God saw fit to heed our prayers."

"What about the people who came to this camp?" Jackson said. "Didn't you tell them you could heal the sick?"

"No. I only talked and prayed with them. Should I turn them away without a little kindness word after they'd come so far?"

Jackson sat back in his chair and folded his arms. His face was very red.

Maxwell drew a deep breath and tried again. "Jane, please look at this our way. In a time of danger, you tell us God has told you to save our people. Don't you see this is difficult to believe?"

"Yes," Jane said, "if I didn't know it to be true, I'd find it hard to believe."

"So help us!" Jackson said. "Give us a sign so we can believe too!"

"Send me to fight and you'll get a sign," Jane said. "Victory."

"So if God will provide this victory, then there's no need for our men. Perhaps we can just send you!"

"No. Our men must fight, and God will give them victory."

Jackson now looked as angry as the night before.

Maxwell said, "Jane, I'm sure you believe . . . all this, but ask yourself: If God wanted someone to fight the Government, wouldn't He choose someone who already knows how to do that?"

"Don't know," she said. "God didn't explain. I sure wouldn't have picked me. So maybe He wants us to turn to Him for strength."

"May I ask a question?" Campbell said. Jackson glared at him. Maxwell sat back, looking relieved. Winslow just stared at the table.

"Jane, if you were to lead our men," Campbell said, "what would you do with them?"

"Attack. Attack now," she said. "Better today than tomorrow. Better tomorrow than the next day."

Jackson narrowed his eyes and shouted, "Attack, attack, attack! This sounds like the Gospel according to Colonel John Campbell. Can't you see that we can't fight the Government? They are too strong. We have to negotiate."

"The Government doesn't negotiate," Campbell said. "It conquers. We need to hit them before--"

"Please!" Winslow said, "Please, gentlemen. We've had this argument too many times." He looked ill and rubbed the sides of his head with his fingertips. "This is a very difficult matter. Very difficult. I have to think . . ."

Jane stood up, leaned forward, her hands flat on the table, and said, "You must decide. We must act now. Do not lose this chance."

As Winslow stared at her, he hunched down in his chair. He looked as though he wanted to be anywhere else but here. To be anyone else than who he was. What we had suspected was true. He was nothing like his father. I was frightened.

After a long moment, Winslow gathered himself and sat up in his chair. He thanked Jane for coming and told her they would be talking again soon.

He nodded to Campbell and Jackson and left the room. Maxwell followed him.

Jane stood at the table and, turning, watched Winslow until he was out the door. Then she looked at me. I could feel her disappointment. We went out of the room, leaving Campbell and Jackson still at the table, still glaring at one another.

9

Jane and I walked to her cabin. She went in and closed the door. Riley was outside, sitting in the sun, cleaning his rifle. I sat next to him. He didn't ask, and I didn't want to tell him what I'd seen. But I reckoned he needed to know. When I was done, all he said was, "Well . . . damn."

Jane stayed inside until we joined her for the evening meal. Riley tried to cheer her up with some of his funny stories. He was in the middle of the one about his Uncle Dewey, a whiskey still, and a skunk when there was a knock on the door.

It was Campbell.

We dished him up a plate of food, and we ate in silence. Campbell was the last to finish. When he pushed back his plate, he said, "I'm here because we have to work together."

We said nothing.

He said to Jane, "First, I don't know if you're talking with God. And I don't care. What I do know is you want to save our people. That's all I care about."

Jane gave a slow nod.

"Second, I want to show you something. Let's clear the table." Afterward, Campbell took a folded map from his coat and opened it on the table. "This is the United States of America before the Plague. Three thousand miles across. Three hundred million people."

Riley let out one of his low whistles.

"After the Plague," Campbell said, "it broke into pieces like a pot dropped on the floor. A thousand pieces. A thousand bands like ours. Some larger and some smaller. We've fought and traded with the bands around us for years: the groups around Asheville, the Tennesseans, the Cherokees, all the little bands up the Shenandoah Valley. Now our problem isn't the other bands. It's the so-called Restored Government. It wants to reclaim all of the old United States."

"All of it?" Riley said. "All three thousand miles?"

"Yes, all of it. They already have almost everything to the north and east of us. The key is the big roads, the Interstate Highways, which the old government built." He pointed out the network of thicker lines on the map, each marked with a number inside a little shield.

"If the Government wants all of this back, it needs these roads to move soldiers, weapons, and supplies."

He pointed to a road that went through the middle of our land. "We've always just called this the big road. We've used it for years to trade with Tennessee and Asheville. But before the Plague it was called Interstate Highway 40, or I-40. It was the southernmost highway through these eastern mountains, our mountains."

"I been in the rocks way above the road," Riley said. "A man with a good rifle could shoot up anything down there. Put enough men up there and we'll stop their army."

"Yes, and they know that," Campbell said. "That's why the Government wants to control the high ground around the road."

"But there are a lot of roads through the mountains," I said. "We use them all the time."

"There are many little winding roads, but the Government's trucks need broad, straight roads. Besides, the little roads are falling apart. After every storm, some piece of them washes out or collapses. It's no matter to us. We're afoot or on horseback and go around. But their trucks can't."

"Couldn't we do that to the big road, damage it so the Government can't use it anymore?" Jane said.

Campbell said, "We can cause landslides blocking the road, but those can be cleared. The Government has machines for that."

"So what do we do?" Jane said.

"Jackson and others on the Council want to negotiate with the Government. Not many people know this, but the Government has offered us a deal. We rejoin the United States, pay taxes, and the Government won't interfere in our local affairs. But we have to disband the militia and give up our guns."

Riley snorted. "Once we can't fight back, why should they keep their side of the bargain?"

"That's right. And Jackson knows that. He doesn't trust the Government. He just doesn't believe we can fight them and win. That's why he wants to negotiate."

"Can we win?" I said.

"Yes," Jane said. "We must."

Campbell nodded. "Yes, but the Government has tens of thousands of soldiers. Its weapons are getting better all the time. All we have are old rifles."

"But we've got the mountains," Riley said. "We know the ground. They don't."

"True," Campbell said. "But we can't hold ground, not against their weapons, not against their numbers."

"If we can't hold ground, what do we do?" I said.

"Attack," Campbell said. "But we have to attack the right way. Instead of going at their strength, we hit and run. We use squads of six or eight men, usually at night. Fast surprise attacks against weak points. Then run and hide. If they come after us, we ambush them. We know how to do that. We've been ambushing raiders for years."

"So where are they weak?" I said.

"A big army needs lots of food, ammunition, medicine, and other supplies. We hit their supplies. We hit the places where they sleep and eat. We'll steal some of their weapons and hit them even harder."

"So won't they just guard those places?" Riley said.

"Sure, but every soldier on guard is one less soldier invading our land. So they need more soldiers, and more supplies, to do the job. If they are always watching their back, they'll be cautious. Moving slow. So we can be that much quicker."

He pointed at the map again. "See these other roads: 81, 77, 26, 85, 75. See how they connect. They give the Government a way around us. From what we hear, they're fighting all over this map. So we have to raise the cost of taking our land, until it's just not worth it. I hope they'll just go around us, leave us alone. At least for a while."

"OK. We can cause trouble and slow them down," I said. "But can we stop them?"

"Yes, if we make their soldiers afraid," Campbell said.

I was puzzled. Riley's eyebrows went up, but Jane just sat listening.

"We fight for our families, our land, and for our lives," Campbell said.

"And for God," Jane said.

"Right," Campbell said. "But most government soldiers are forced to fight. If they refuse, they're punished, even killed. So we kill these unwilling men with raids and ambushes. Their fear of us, their fear of dying, dying for nothing, will grow. We have to make them fear us more than they fear the Government. I believe we can beat an army, even a big army, of fearful men."

"So what do you want us to do?" Riley said.

Campbell pointed to Riley and me and said, "Keep her alive. No matter what."

We nodded.

He turned to Jane. "You have to make our people and our men believe we can win."

Riley let out one of his low whistles. "Now, don't make it too easy on her Colonel."

Campbell said, "Jane, I can't tell you how to do that. We could try this, but I don't think we can win without you."

Jane looked at him. "If it's God's will, He'll make a way. I just have to be ready."

"My job is to convince Winslow to do this rather than negotiate," Campbell said. "And I'll tell you straight, I don't know how I'm going to do that."

"There's one thing I have to know," Jane said. "If Winslow says no, will you do it anyway?"

"No. I'll not divide our people. That would be fatal."

"Then I'm with you," Jane said, "even though you don't believe God is in this." Then she added, "Colonel, I'll pray for you. I'll pray you find a way to convince Winslow."

Campbell looked a little surprised, as if he didn't know what to say. Then he said, "Thank you."

He stood up, folded his map, and put it back in his coat. Wishing us a good night, he went out. The three of us sat around the table. Silent. Thinking about war.

10

The next morning, Jane came out of her cabin and screamed at Riley and me, "Come! Hurry!" Then she was running toward the main building.

We grabbed our rifles and scrambled after her. As we ran to catch up, I looked around expecting to see the camp under attack. But it was a quiet morning, the smoke of little cooking fires reaching up toward the sky, a few men moving about.

Up ahead, Jane was running as hard as she could, kicking up dust from the path. Riley and I were still ten yards behind when a startled guard shouted, "Stop right there!" and pointed his rifle at Jane.

She stopped, dropped her rifle, and raised her hands. "Get Winslow out of that building! Get everyone out of there! Hurry!"

The guard froze, not knowing what to do. Then he saw Riley and me running up, rifles in hand. He backed up a step and shouted, "Stop!" His finger moved to the trigger.

Riley and I stopped a few steps behind Jane. "Take it easy," I said as calmly as I could. We put our rifles down and raised our hands. The guard's eyes bounced back and forth between us.

"Take it easy," I said again.

I glanced toward the building. Every guard had a gun on us. A Lieutenant, his pistol drawn, was walking toward us. "What's going on here?" he said.

Jane shouted again. "Get Winslow out! He's in danger! Get everyone out! Now!"

The Lieutenant didn't know what to make of this girl shouting at him. He glanced down the hill. The camp was quiet. No movement. No alarms. Nothing. "Danger? What kind of danger?" he said.

Before Jane could say anything, I said, "Call Campbell."

The Lieutenant looked at me, and then at Jane. Turning back to the porch, he called out. "Get Colonel Campbell."

We all just stood and waited. Jane looked to the east, then at the entrance to the building, then east again. I looked east too. All I saw was the camp below us, and the sun coming up behind the mountains. It looked to be a nice day.

I was about to ask Jane what this was about when Campbell came out.

"Lieutenant," he called out, "let her come up. The other two are OK. Stand down." Jane ran to Campbell. Riley picked up Jane's rifle and his own. I got mine.

I couldn't hear what Jane said to Campbell, but she pointed to the east. He listened, said something to her, and looked east. Then he went back inside the building, leaving Jane on the porch. She stood looking east. I turned and looked that way again. Nothing.

The guard who had stopped us said, "What's going on?"

"Don't know," Riley said. "But listen. You ever point a weapon at her again, we'll kill you."

The guard looked at Riley. Then at me. I nodded.

A minute later, Campbell came out on the porch with Jackson and Winslow. Again, I couldn't hear them. Jane spoke with the same gestures and pointed east. The three men looked and saw nothing, nothing but the rising sun and mountains.

They all turned back to her. Campbell's face was blank. As usual, Jackson was angry. Winslow looked concerned, as though Jane was a child frightened by a nightmare. He was reaching out to touch her shoulder when I heard it, when we all heard it.

It was that distant humming sound. An airplane. But it was different from before. Deeper in tone and pulsing. We looked in the sky trying to locate it. Three spots in front of the sun. Three airplanes. They were different from the one we saw in the meadow. Larger. Louder. Faster.

For a second, no one moved. Then shouts of "Cover!" Someone started ringing a bell to alarm the camp.

I saw Jane and the others rushing off the porch. I could hear the humming of the airplanes get louder. The guards were firing at them with their rifles.

I was turning to run toward Jane, when someone ran into me, knocking me down. I rolled down the hill a few yards and then scrambled to my feet. Confused, I didn't know which way to run. The guards were shooting up into the sky. Then there was a flash, and I felt something hit me all over, all at once.

Next, I was laying flat on my belly, my face in the dirt. I felt the earth heave, then heave again, and again. I curled up in a ball, my hands over my ears. I don't remember thinking or feeling anything except fear. Perhaps I was screaming. I just tightened myself into a fist.

The heaving stopped. My ears were ringing, but I could still hear someone close by shrieking. The sound of pain.

I could see nothing, nothing but a cloud of choking dust and smoke. Then I put my head down and let everything disappear.

When I came to, I rolled over and got to my feet. I wasn't hurt, but I felt slow in the head. Stunned. But the smoke and dust had cleared enough for me to see. The front of the building had been turned into rubble. Some of it burning. A group of men placed another man, bloody, twisting, and screaming, on a plank. They carried him down the hill.

Pieces of paper were scattered all around me. I picked one up. One side of the paper had two drawings. The top drawing showed a woman with a baby walking toward the door of a house. She was walking away from what I guessed was government soldier. He wore a black uniform with the old American flag on the sleeve. Below this, the words: CITIZENS - STAY IN YOUR HOMES.

The bottom drawing showed another soldier pointing his rifle at a man whose hands were raised over his head. Under this, MILITIA – DO NOT RESIST.

On the other side of paper was a picture of the old flag with the words, RESTORING THE GREATNESS OF OUR NATION.

Jane ran up to me. She said, "You hurt?"

"No, just got knocked around some. You?"

"Not a scratch."

"What about the others? Riley?"

"Safe."

Jane picked up one of the papers. She looked at the drawings for a moment and flipped it over. "The airplanes dropped these. What's it say?" I read it to her. She said nothing.

I looked around the camp and saw many little groups, all gathered around someone who could read. The last few papers fluttered out of the trees. We stood there for a while, quiet. I said to Jane, "This'll be worse than anything since the Plague."

"May God forgive them," Jane said. "I'll never."

"Jane, you sure you want to do this? You sure you want to go to war?"

"You don't understand," she said. "I was born for this."

11

I heard a voice behind me say, "Hey." Turning, I saw an old man, a tangled white beard halfway down his skinny chest. He said, "Which way, son?"

"Yonder," I said, pointing through the trees to a crowd of men sitting on the ground waiting for the prayer service to begin, waiting to be sent off to fight. The old man squinted in that direction, maybe having trouble seeing that far. "Obliged," he said and limped away, using his rifle for support.

Nobody had told them to come. In the days after the attack, they would just arrive in ones and twos. Most were men who had done their time in the militia. Others were men who had drifted home, deserted. Now they had come back to fight the Government, no questions asked. Their courage made me proud. Was courage enough? But that was about all we had.

I went and found a place among the men sitting on the ground. Winslow, Jackson, Campbell, and Reverend Maxwell sat on benches down in the front. And then there was Jane. She sat at Winslow's side. She looked better in the new britches and coat Winslow had gotten made for her. The men around me gawked at her.

Maxwell stood and told us we would begin by singing David Winslow's favorite hymn. He didn't have to tell us what it was. Although we had pretty much stopped singing it when he died, the words came back to us. We sang, "Onward, Christian soldiers, marching as to war, / With the cross of Jesus going on before. / Christ, the royal Master, leads against the foe; / Forward into battle see His banners go!" Our voices got louder as we went and we had the old feeling again. At the end, Maxwell said a prayer and had us sit down. Then he read from the Bible.

It was a war story from Second Chronicles, Chapter 20. A big army was coming to attack the people of Judah. King Jehoshaphat assembled his people and appealed to God for help against their enemies. "O our God, wilt thou not judge them? For we have no might against this great company that cometh against us; neither know we what to do: but our eyes are upon thee."

And God spoke through a man in the assembly. "Thus saith the LORD unto you, Be not afraid nor dismayed by reason of this great multitude; for the battle is not yours, but God's."

King Jehoshaphat and the people had faith. So God was with them and destroyed their enemies. "And when Judah came toward the watch tower in the wilderness, they looked unto the multitude, and, behold, they were dead bodies fallen to the earth, and none escaped." The people of Judah went down and stripped the dead bodies of anything of value. "And they were three days in gathering of the spoil, it was so much."

I tried to imagine it. All those bloating bodies stinking in the sun. Clouds of flies. Huge swarms of them. Scavenger birds ripping out eyeballs, tearing at soft bits of flesh, eating their fill. And the victors, celebrating, praising God while robbing the dead.

When he finished reading, I expected Maxwell to start preaching, but instead he said, "Let us pray." He prayed first for the men who were killed and wounded in the airplane attack. Then he said, "Please bless the Leader of our people, General Winslow. Give him the wisdom to lead us in this war for our freedom. Bless also the Messenger you have sent to us, our sister Jane. Continue to speak through her to provide light in this dark time. And Lord, bless these brave men who go forth into the storm of battle. Give them the strength and the courage to do your will. In the name of Jesus. Amen."

When we opened our eyes and looked up, Winslow was standing before us, holding a sheet of paper. His hand was shaking, just enough to be noticeable.

He cleared his throat and began to speak, looking down at his piece of paper. I could just barely hear him, and soon he was interrupted by shouts of "Can't hear!" and "Speak up!" Winslow looked up, startled. He cleared his throat and began again, a little louder.

"Men. I only want to say a few things. First, I want to thank all of you for your courage during the attack . . . and since then. Our people can be proud of you."

"Second, the enemy we now face is unlike any we have faced in the past. They have new weapons . . . . So, . . . we are going to have to fight them in new ways. We'll be providing you with more details soon. . . ."

Bored, men began plucking at the grass or and looking up at the sky. I saw some men whispering to others.

Winslow looked down at his paper and then back at us. "I'm sure you've all heard about this young woman and . . . um . . . what she has done. But before she speaks to you, I want to offer her a token of my gratitude and respect."

He gestured to Jane to stand next to him as someone brought him a rifle. At first glance, it appeared just like any other, scarred with age and hard use. Then we all saw it. The letters "DW" had been burned into the wooden stock. David Winslow's rifle.

Winslow cleared his throat and said to Jane. "This is my father's rifle. Um . . . I want you to carry it." He handed the rifle to Jane. We all began to clap. He seemed surprised. Giving her that rifle was generous and noble. Only later did I see how much he must have regretted it.

Jane held the rifle as if it were a newborn child. Then grasping it with one hand, she lifted it high over her head in a gesture of strength. She smiled. It was a smile of triumph and joy, as though her war had already been won. We leapt to our feet and clapped even louder.

After a long moment, she motioned for us to sit down.

"General Winslow," she said, her voice clear and strong. "Thank you. It will be an honor to carry the rifle of a great man of God."

There was applause again. When it died down, she said, "I am Jane Darcy. I've been safe my whole life cause of men like you. You've slept on the cold ground, gone hungry, and lived with danger and death. For this, your mothers, your sisters, your wives, your daughters, and I, thank you.

"Now God has called me to be a Messenger. I don't know how to fight. But I know we must fight. We must win. And we will win!"

We roared our approval. We'd found someone who believed, who could make us believe again. Charles Winslow and his shaking hands were forgotten.

"Why did God call me, a girl who knows nothing of war? I don't know. But maybe by picking someone so weak, He's saying we must depend on Him, not ourselves, for strength.

"Yes, strength. We'll need His strength against this new and terrible enemy. They call themselves the Restored Government of the United States. They wave the old flag. They claim to be America. But we know it's a lie. The old Government fought for justice. But these liars fight to conquer and enslave. The old flag stood for freedom. But their flag stands for power. America was a nation under God. But our enemy hates God.

"Yes, strength. We'll need His strength. We've seen what their bombs can do, and the Spirit has shown me there are more to come. Remember what the Bible says, 'Be not afraid, for the battle is not ours, but God's.' Face the enemy and the Lord will be with us."

She lifted the rifle and again we roared.

"To protect our people, we must be pure. You must not swear, gamble, drink, or break any of the Commandments. And you must be chaste. In all ways, you must be upright men of God. I know this will be difficult. But to win the outward battle, we must first win the inward battle. If we sin, God will permit us to lose this war. If we sin, God will turn His face from us."

For a long moment, she was silent. Letting it sink in. We were silent too, waiting for her next word.

"This is the most important thing. You must believe with all your heart this war is a holy cause. A holy cause. You must become God's Army. And to be a weapon in the hands of God, you must give everything."

She paused, letting the silence collect and become powerful like water behind a dam. Then she shouted, "I ask you: Will you give everything?"

We shouted "YES!"

"I ask you: Will you fight?"

"YES!"

"I ask you: Will you win?"

"YES!"

Jane looked at us in silence for a long moment. Then she lifted one clenched fist above her head and shouted, "Say after me: In the name of God!"

We each raised a fist and shouted, "IN THE NAME OF GOD!"

"For our people!"

"FOR OUR PEOPLE!"

"For our land!"

"FOR OUR LAND!"

"We will prevail!"

"WE WILL PREVAIL!"

"Once more," she shouted. "We will prevail!"

We roared it back to her, "WE WILL PREVAIL!" And then we cheered, slapped one another on the back, and threw our hats in the air. Tears of joy in our eyes. We wanted to go to war. We wanted to be God's weapon. To give everything. In that moment, she could have sent us charging down from the mountains at the enemy.

We belonged to her.

12

Riley asked me to write a letter for him. He wasn't planning to send it. With all that was happening, it would be foolish to do that. He would keep the letter in his coat pocket. If something happened, it would tell who he was. Maybe somebody would get the letter to his folks. "Don't know why I should bother," Riley said, "not much chance it'd ever get home."

"If it comes to that," I said, "I'll tell them."

"Thanks."

"Just do the same for me."

"Sure."

"What do you want to say?"

I wrote it down. It wasn't much. I read it back to him, and asked if he wanted to add anything. He sat quiet for a bit and then shook his head. Then I showed him how to make the letters, and he put his name at the bottom. We folded the paper. On the outside, I wrote the name of his folks and the place they lived

He put it in a pocket. We sat, saying nothing, for a while. Then Riley said he was going visiting around camp. He walked off into the dark.

I sat at the fire and thought about writing a letter for myself. It was hard to get started. But before I'd written a word, a man came out of the darkness. He said Riley told him I knew writing, and he wanted a letter too. When we were done, two other men came. Then another and another. And so on.

They all had a hangdog look, a little ashamed they had to ask for help, and even more ashamed to tell a stranger their thoughts. Most were like Riley, saying only a little. A couple went on for a while.

When the last one was gone, it was late and I was tired. I wondered if I should bother with a letter. Riley had been right. A scrap of paper had little chance of getting back to my folks. All those men knew the same thing. The letter was next to useless. Maybe they just wanted to say the secret things in their hearts, just wanted to know those things could be summoned up, said aloud, put on paper, made real.

I took out another piece of paper and sat looking at the faint blue lines in the firelight. In the end, I only wrote my name, the names of my parents, and where we lived. I didn't see the need for more. Perhaps I would later. I put my things away, laid out my bedroll, and looked at Jane's cabin. A lamp was still burning. She was awake.

How she could be so sure about what God wanted? I didn't know. Was she right about any of it?

Anyway, I thought, I've made my choice.

13

I peered over the rocks at the soldiers as they came to the bend in the trail. Eight weary men in black uniforms walking single file. Most were looking down. They weren't watching for an ambush. Their thoughts were somewhere else.

As I watched them come on, the last few moments seemed to stretch, to fill hours. I could hear the rustling sound of branches overhead moved by a breeze. Sunshine felt hot on my neck, the grain of the rock rough on my cheek. A butterfly flew across the trail, ignoring the men in black, ignoring us.

Our squad leader hit the first one in the chest, right of center. The soldier spun around, sinking to the ground. Watching him go down, the rest of them froze.

Then we all started shooting. I hit one of them in the chest. He dropped his rifle but didn't go down right away. For an instant, he looked at the blood spurting out of him. Then he went to his knees and fell forward. After he was down, I fired again but didn't hit anything.

It was over in seconds. Only one soldier managed to use his automatic rifle, spraying bullets. The noise of his weapon was deafening. But he only hit trees, showering us with splinters and dust. Then one of us shot him. My ears rang in the sudden quiet.

It was Jane's first fight. Crouching next to me behind a rock, she had fired her rifle. But I don't know if she hit anyone. When the shooting stopped, she stood up. I pulled her down until I was sure it was safe. Only when our squad leader gave the all-clear did we go down to look at bodies

The first man I came to had a bloody hole where his nose used to be. He was bent backward over a rock, eyes open, looking up through the trees at sky. The rest of them lay sprawled and twisted on the rocky ground.

There was blood splattered about, and it was beginning to pool around the bodies. The first flies were arriving.

As we moved down from the rocks, I kept Jane behind me. I jumped a little when I heard a single shot off to my right. It was just one of our men finishing off a soldier. The squad leader said to the man, "Don't waste bullets. Use your knife." As usual, we began stripping the bodies of anything useful. And we picked up our own shell casings so they could be reloaded.

Jane sat on a rock, looking at the dead.

I was watching her when Riley came up beside me. "How's she doing?"

"Better than me the first time," I said.

We went up to her. She looked at us. "So this is it."

"Yeah," I said. "This is it."

Jane got down off the rock. She went over to a dead soldier and knelt down next to him. I wondered if she had killed him. I didn't ask.

She hesitated before reaching up to close the dead man's eyes. Gently. Then she started going through his pockets.

The Government's army came up the big road like a giant snake, slowly swallowing every turn and every town along the road. From a distance, you could hear the artillery and bombs, the clatter of the big .50 caliber machine guns. And we fought back Campbell's way--ambushes, hit-and-run attacks, blocking roads with felled trees and rockslides. We didn't hold ground, but we could draw blood.

It was easy enough to do. The soldiers weren't that good at fighting, not against us anyway. Most seemed stupid and lazy. Some would turn and run at the first sign of trouble, or hide until the shooting was over. I suppose they didn't want to die for nothing. Our people found the soldiers were willing to trade food, equipment, and even information for homebrewed whiskey.

Still, I wasn't so sure it would work against all the weapons and all the men the government had. But it wasn't my job to figure that out. My job was to keep Jane alive.

At first, I thought that might be easy. Back at Central Camp, Winslow told Jane she had to stay away from the fighting, that she was too important.

"Winslow," she said, "That's the most fool thing I've ever heard. I have to fight."

Well, everybody in the room got real quiet. Nobody talked that way to Winslow. He was used to folks calling him "General" and kissing his ass. Now Jane had gone and called him a fool right to his face. He just sat there, blinking with surprise.

She crossed her arms, leaned back in her chair, and glared at him. I was reminded of an old horse that's decided it was done with plowing. Not another inch.

In the end, Campbell talked Winslow into letting Jane visit our men, who were to be scattered in small units throughout the mountains. Riley and I would go along to protect her. I guess Winslow thought this was safe. But it wasn't. It meant Jane could go anywhere she wanted. And she wanted to go where nothing was safe.

Jane would decide where to go, and we would hook up with the militia unit in that area. Usually, this meant going out with a squad, hiding with them in the trees beside a road, and waiting for some government trucks to come along. We would shoot them up, trying to kill drivers and damage the engines or the wheels, and running off before they started shooting back. If any of them were stupid enough to chase us, we would hide and ambush them.

Jane had no rank, but she carried David Winslow's rifle and supposedly talked with God. The men were always raising one clenched fist to her as a kind of salute. She nodded in return. Maybe those men didn't really believe God guided her, yet I never saw anyone refuse her a thing.

I don't know how else to say it, but Jane had a kind of glow about her in those early days. It wasn't something you could see with your eyes. She was as dirty, hungry, and beat up as the rest of us. But she believed God's promises were being fulfilled. Victory was coming. I think she believed it the way you and I believe the sun will come up tomorrow.

You might think men were just curious about her. Sure, a girl who talks to God and carries a rifle was an odd thing, a thing you would go out of your way to see. But there was more to it than that. And it wasn't like the way girls draw boys by being pretty or clever. We were drawn because she was so sure, dead certain, about everything.

I think ordinary folk, like you and I, always have a pinch of doubt mixed into our certainty. We don't ever know, not for a fact, everything we need to know. Of course, you have to do something. You just have to be sure enough.

Like playing cards. You might have a good hand, but the other fellow might have better. You don't know. There are times, of course, when you have to bet heavy to win. But if you're smart, you don't do it often. And if you can, you hold a little back for the next hand. Only a fool bets everything every time the cards are dealt.

Only a fool. Or someone like Jane.

You could see this in the way she gave us hell for Sin, breaking any of the Commandments. Any of them. She had told us to be upright men of God or God would turn His face from our people, and she damn well meant it. To most folks there are big sins and little sins. And most folks don't worry too much about the little ones. Jane wasn't like that.

Once, she came across a few of our boys having a little whiskey. It wasn't like they were drunk or getting wild. They weren't neglecting their duty or anything. They were just having a few sips. I didn't see the harm in it. But she did.

Before they could say a thing, Jane grabbed their whiskey bottle and smashed it against a tree.

Enraged, one man took off his hat and threw it down. He shouted at her, "What call you got to do that?"

"You know," she said.

"We wasn't doing no harm."

She took a step forward and glared at him, and he glared right back. But after a moment, he looked down at his boots. The other men did the same thing. Jane stood there a little longer before she turned and walked off.

Now you shouldn't think she was always shouting at us or raising hell. She wasn't. In fact, she didn't go for preaching at all, unless something like drinking or cursing set her off. One thing she would always do was sit and pray with any wounded or dying men. That was hard on her. She would come away from that looking worn down. But most times, she would sit at a fire with our men and listen to them talk about the fighting, about what worked against the soldiers and what didn't. And she would laugh at a funny story just as hard as anybody else. It would have been enough for us if she had simply gone along, shared all the hard things without complaint. Our men felt better because Jane was there. Her faith in victory was like a fire. We crowded around her, warming ourselves against the cold facts of life and death.

Of course, warming yourself at a fire is a passing thing. Go about your business and you get cold again. And that might have been all there was to Jane--the strange girl who made us feel better for a time. But Jane became more than that.

One time Riley and I were sitting with some men. Jane must've been talking to an officer or the squad leader. One of the men asked us if it was true what he had heard.

"Depends," Riley said. "What'd you hear?"

I expected the man was talking about healing the little girl, or about how Jane had known the government airplanes were coming. But the man said he had heard Jane had run into machine gun fire and carried a wounded man out, saving his life.

"She sure did," Riley said. "Saw it myself." Then he looked over at me with a little smile, like this was real funny, and said, "Ain't that right partner?"

I couldn't make a liar out of Riley, even if he wasn't telling the truth. So I nodded.

This is how it really happened. We were coming down a rocky slope toward a road when soldiers started shooting at us from the woods on the far side. I jumped behind a rock and looked for Jane. She was to my right and had enough cover. Riley was on the other side of her and looked OK.

I shucked off my bedroll and rose up a little. I fired a shot in the general direction of the soldiers, worked the bolt, and fired again. Bullets started hitting nearby, and I made myself as small as I could behind the rock. Then the shooting stopped. It was very quiet for a moment, but then I heard the screaming. It was one of our men. He was sprawled near the road's edge. Blood was pouring out of his belly, and he was screaming for help, screaming something terrible for us to come get him. The soldiers, of course, would cut down anyone crazy enough to try that. I thought one of us should just shoot him, put him out of his misery, but I didn't want to do it.

I heard Jane shout, "We've got to help him." But when I turned toward her, all I saw was her bedroll. She was running downhill toward the road. The soldiers started shooting again.

Riley and I started after her. It's hard to explain why we went. Maybe we thought giving the soldiers two more targets would give Jane a better chance. Maybe we couldn't stand doing nothing while she got herself killed.

As I took my first step, I heard our men start shooting, trying to protect Jane. I ran as hard as I could, but tripped, fell, and rolled. By the time I had scrambled to my feet, Jane and Riley had gotten to the wounded man. They were on their bellies trying to drag him into a shallow weedy ditch on the near side of the road. As I ran toward them, I could feel the air around me moving and humming with bullets. It was like running through a swarm of bees without being stung.

I knew at any moment one of the bullets might hit me in the head, blowing my brains out one side. Or one might rip into my guts, or shatter the bones in a leg. Then I would be screaming, bleeding, and dying hard like the poor bastard Jane was trying to help. This was as close to death as I had ever been. So I should have been crazy with fear, shitting-my-pants fear. Instead, I felt laughter coming up from deep down inside, the silly laughter of a boy playing games.

That feeling went away, popped like a soap bubble, when I landed in the ditch. Then I was scared again, dry-as-dust thirsty, guts in knots, my skin trying to crawl off the bones, and my right knee hurting like hell from landing on a rock. I rose up as much as I dared and saw Jane and Riley had the wounded man down in the ditch. He had stopped screaming, and his clothes, neck to knees, were soaked with blood. Jane was next to him, her ear close to his mouth, which was moving a little. Staying low, I crawled in the ditch to them and looked at Riley. He was saying something to me, but I couldn't make it out for all the shooting.

"What?" I shouted and cupped a hand at my ear.

"Glad you could make it," he shouted and smiled.

I smiled back at him and shouted, "You OK?"

He nodded. I looked at Jane. She appeared unhurt. But with so much blood on her clothes, I wasn't sure. I slapped her on one boot to get her attention. When she looked at me, I shouted, "You OK?" She nodded.

Some shots hit close by, throwing up a bunch of dirt and rocks. I ducked. When I looked up, Riley was wiping the dirt from his face, and there was a little trickle of blood on his forehead. He shouted, "Goddammit!"

"Riley," Jane shouted, just as loud. "Don't curse!"

He looked at her and started laughing. I started laughing too. Jane looked back and forth between us, puzzled. Then she started laughing. We laughed like three crazy people until Riley shouted, "Ready?"

"Go!" I shouted. We popped up, fired at the soldiers, and ducked down again. They fired back, kicking up even more dirt around us.

Riley and I did that for a while: popping up, shooting, and ducking. We knew we had to keep the soldiers shooting at us while some of our men got around behind them. At least, that's what I hoped they were doing.

Jane kept talking to the wounded man, who just stared up at the sky.

Finally, we heard a different kind of shots in the woods across the road. The soldiers stopped firing at us. There was a scream and a few more shots. Then silence.

I reckoned it was over and began to stand up. But Jane screamed, "No!" and waved me down. I took cover. Just then, another burst of fire came out of the woods, slicing through the air just above my head.

When I stood up again, I saw a soldier running out of the trees. He dropped his rifle, and ran straight down the middle of road, pumping his arms and legs real wild. Stupid panic. Riley stood up, took aim, and put a shot into the man's back, a little right of center. The soldier staggered a few steps, fell hard on his knees and hands, and crawled a few feet before collapsing.

Some of our men ran to the ditch to help our wounded man. But he was dead. It was really over now.

My knee hurt, and I felt confused, lightheaded and thirsty. I just wanted to sit down and drink cool water until the spring went dry. Jane stood on the road and watched as our man was carried into the woods to be buried. She was covered in dirt and his blood, but she was unhurt. Then she looked at me and smiled.

She had saved my life, but I was angry. She could've died. What she had done was stupid, crazy. But it was useless to tell her that. Jane was not some excited kid who had to be taught not to take foolish chances. She was something else, something for which I didn't have a name.

So I just said, "Why?"

"Nobody ought to die alone."

I nodded.

So it happened that way. Maybe I should've told those men what I've told you. But I suspect it wouldn't have done any good. The story of Jane saving that man was just too good. And in the telling and retelling, a good story grows and grows into something bigger. The bigger story becomes easier to believe. Then it's too late to go back.

14

We were searching the bodies of soldiers after an ambush and Riley said, "This one's alive." He took a deep breath and pulled out his knife.

"Stop," Jane said. We all looked at her, wondering what the hell she was doing.

We didn't take prisoners. We couldn't. We didn't have any place keep them or spare men to guard them. We had to kill them or leave them to die of their wounds. But not this time.

A bullet had creased the soldier's skull, knocking him cold. Jane had us haul him away, bound and blindfolded, of course, to the cellar of an old house. Somebody put some bandages on his head wound, but it wasn't until the next day that he woke up. Then he raised all kinds of hell, trying to get loose, shouting and cursing. The only time he shut up was when somebody fed him.

When Jane went down to talk to him, he was sitting slumped forward in a chair, his hands bound behind him. His uniform was dirty and torn. As we walked down the creaking stairs, he lifted his blindfolded head. His mouth was set a hard thin line.

Jane sent the men who were guarding him upstairs and took off the prisoner's blindfold. He squinted and blinked getting used to even the dim lamplight in the cellar. It took a few moments, but finally he got a good look at Jane.

"Who the fuck are you?" His voice sounded dry.

Jane asked Riley to get some water and a clean cloth. After cleaning his face, she gave him a long drink of water. Then she sat down facing him.

"Who the fuck are you?" he said.

I wanted to hit him, teach him some manners, and took a step forward. Riley was doing the same. But Jane gave us a look that said, No.

"I have some questions," she said.

"Marcus Hobbes, First Lieutenant, U.S. Army, serial number 58932923."

"My name is Jane Darcy. God has called me to save my people from their enemy, the United States."

Laughing, he said, "You Hillbillies are crazy."

"Don't you believe in God, Lieutenant Hobbes?"

"No," he said and spat on the floor at her feet. There was blood in his spittle.

"Why not?"

"What did your God do about the Plague? Nothing. What has God done since then? Nothing. God's a story for children. God's a joke. There is no God. We're on our own."

I expected her to argue. Instead, she just said, "Why are you doing this?"

"Doing what?" He sounded a little unsure.

"Taking our land."

"We're not taking your land. We're the Government of the United States of America. This is U.S. territory. If you resist lawful authority, we have to use force."

"You don't really believe that, do you?"

"We're the Government of--"

"That government died 26 years ago."

"We're rebuilding. The United States of America was a great nation. And it can be again."

"And you're going to get it all back, from ocean to ocean?"

"Yes, from ocean to ocean. One nation."

"What if we don't want to be part of your nation?"

"They all say the same thing." He spat again on the floor.

"We're different. We'll fight for our freedom. God is--"

He laughed and said, "Another freedom fighter. They all say that too."

Again, I expected her to argue, but she only said, "So when everyone is forced to be in your nation, what then Lieutenant?"

"What do you mean?"

"Once you conquer everyone you call 'Americans,' you'll be very powerful. But will you have a great nation?"

"Before the Plague," he said, "Three hundred million Americans were the richest people on earth. Now there's only thirty or forty million and most wonder if they'll survive the next winter. You know why?"

"Tell me."

"There's no law and order. Law and order make everything possible. I'm from New York City. Ever heard of it?"

Jane nodded.

"Before the Plague," he said, "New York was the biggest, richest city in

America. After, it was hell on earth. Worse than any hell your damn preachers can invent. I've seen things you can't imagine."

Jane just sat, waiting for him to go on.

"All we had was hunger and fear," he said. "For years, we were nothing but animals. Then the Government came. It fed us. Soldiers gave me my first decent meal, my first warm coat. The Government started schools. I learned to read and write. Do you know how to do that girl?"

She shook her head.

"Of course, you don't," he said. "The government of the United States did that for me, for millions of us. It gave us a future. And how? Law and order. Law and order make it possible to walk down a street without fear of being robbed or raped or murdered. Law and order make it possible to grow crops and to build factories. Law and order will make America a great nation again."

"So that's it," she said, "law and order?"

"Yes. In Government territory, we have schools, roads, hospitals, and even some electricity. You ignorant Hillbillies ought to beg us to become citizens again. Instead, you fight us." He spat on the floor.

"Why do you think we fight?"

"Too fucking stupid and backward to know better."

"No. We just want to be free."

"Freedom is bullshit," he said. "Right now, you're free to be hungry, free to be ignorant, and free to die young."

"Our lives are hard, but there's no one giving us orders, telling us how to live."

"Somebody's always giving orders. Without those orders, people will tear each other apart like starving rats. I know. I've seen it. Your Charles Winslow gives orders and your preachers tell you how to live. If you ask them why, they'll say, 'God says.' But when we tell you how to live, we don't hide behind a lie."

"God is not a lie."

"Oh, that's right," he said, laughing. "You talk with God."

She glared at him.

"Tell me this," he said. "When this is over, won't Winslow and the preachers tell you, 'Go home little girl, fuck your cousin, and make babies?'"

I wanted to hit the bastard, smash his head.

"And they'll say," he continued, "'God wants it that way.'"

She didn't say anything. It was the first time I had ever seen someone shut her up.

"But is that what you want?" he said. "Do you really want to be barefoot and pregnant in a cold, filthy shack for the rest of your life?"

"What I want is nothing. Only God's will matters."

"You just proved my point. The preachers have you fooled. Completely fooled."

"Lieutenant, you don't know anything about God or my people. And you don't know anything about me, or about what I want. I know what God requires of me."

"Well, I do know you people always kill your prisoners. So sooner or later, one of you will shoot me in the back of the head or cut my throat. So fuck you and fuck God. Fuck all of you."

Jane sat looking at him with a sad expression. Then she looked away and sat up straight as though she were somewhere else, listening to a voice only she could hear.

She stood up and told Riley to put the blindfold back on Hobbes. Then she grabbed me by the arm and charged up the stairs.

"Come on," she said. "We've got to write a letter."

I wrote down what she said. I had to stop her often because I couldn't keep up. When she finished, I read it back to her. She changed nothing.

This is what the letter said.

> To the So-Called Restored USA:
>
> My name is Jane. God sent me to protect my people and to bring you a Message. Go home. Leave us alone. We have a God-given right to be free. We have God's law. We do not need your law and order. Do not die to enslave us. Do not die in an unjust cause. If you do not believe God's Message, you will die. God is with us and against you. If you obey God, you will be forgiven.
>
> Go home. Leave us alone. Do not die and be damned for eternity.
>
> IN THE NAME OF GOD, WE WILL PREVAIL

When we were done, I copied it out as neat as I could. I asked Jane how she planned to send it to the Government.

"The prisoner," she said.

"The prisoner?"

"Remember what David Winslow did with the man he didn't hang? He sent that man to spread the word. That's what we'll do with Lieutenant Hobbes. We'll send him back with the letter."

"Jane, are you sure? He probably knows a lot. Shouldn't we make him tell us about what their army is doing? And, I don't know, their weapons and such."

"Remember what Jesus was always saying to the disciples?"

"What?"

"O Ye of little faith." She picked up the letter and went to tell the officer in charge of the militia unit what she wanted.

Then Jane and I went back to the cellar. I removed Hobbes's blindfold.

"We're letting you go," she said. "Deliver this letter to your leaders."

"Letter?" he said, blinking in the light.

She held up the folded page and put it in his shirt pocket. "Deliver my letter. Tell them about me. Tell them what I said. I want them to know God has sent a Messenger."

"What's the trick?"

"No trick," Jane said. "We let you go, and then you get back to your army. Deliver the letter. Tell them about me. Do your duty."

He narrowed his eyes as if trying to see what was wrong with this.

Two men came. They put the blindfold back on Hobbes and took him up the stairs.

I heard Hobbes shout, "Hey Jane! Jane Darcy!" He must've wanted to say something else to her. But she gave no sign of hearing that, so I let it pass. I wanted to talk to her.

"Are you sure about this?" I said. "Now they'll know who you are and what you look like. The Government will try to get you like it tried to get Winslow with the airplanes."

"That's right," she said.

About two weeks later, someone brought in one of the signs being posted by the soldiers in the towns and villages. It offered a reward for "information leading to the capture 'Jane Darcy.'" The sign said what she looked like and how she wore men's clothing. It also warned she was "armed and dangerous." It had a drawing of her--a squarish face with a mean scowl, framed by short scruffy hair.

When I read what it said to Riley and Jane, they had a good laugh. "Do you think I look like that?" Jane said, pointing to the drawing, "I mean, she's so . . . unfriendly."

"Well," Riley said, "she is armed and dangerous." And they laughed some more.

I didn't think it was funny. Now the Government was hunting her. She was in more danger than ever.

Jane saw I wasn't laughing. "Think what this means," she said. "All the people who see this sign will know I'm not scared of the Government. And then they'll all know they shouldn't be scared either."

I couldn't think of what to say. I knew how to fight. I had killed. Yet I was afraid to die. I could master that fear for a while, but I was still afraid. I understood, at last, she was not.

15

"Hiding it can be a mite tricky," said the man and he began to lay twigs and leaves across the hole he had dug. "Make it look like solid ground, so maybe they'll step there."

At the bottom of the hole was a board with big rusty nails sticking straight up. When a soldier stepped in the hole, the nails would go right through his boot, up into his foot. It hurt just to think about it.

The man looked up at us and smiled. His name was Cosgrove, and he had a friendly face.

"Put some shit on the nails," he said. "Just dip 'em in a pile. Betcha that soldier's foot will swell up bad, maybe have to get cut off. Maybe get the blood poisoning and die. Anyway, one less soldier boy we gotta shoot." He grinned.

Jane had been squatting next to Cosgrove. Standing up, she looked around at us and said, "What's important is making the soldiers afraid, afraid even to walk on our land." Campbell had told us this same thing.

Solemn as deacons, we all nodded our agreement. I wouldn't have been surprised if somebody had said, "Amen." Then Jane squatted again and told Cosgrove to go on. We all leaned in, trying to get a good look.

I turned to say something to Riley. But he wasn't there. I looked around and saw he was leaning up against a tree, away from the crowd. I went over to him. He didn't look happy.

"What's wrong?" I said.

"I wonder if this is such a good idea."

"Why?"

Riley scratched his beard for a moment. "One time I was hunting with Daddy and Uncle Dewey. You remember me talking about Uncle Dewey?"

"Sure. The story about the skunk. But what's this got to do with--"

"Hang on. We was hunting, and our dogs got after this bear. Big old bastard. Six maybe seven hundred pounds. Dogs cornered him. While one dog came from the front, a couple others would tear at the bear's backside. Bear would roar and turn around, but that dog would get out of reach. Then the other dog would go at him from behind. So on."

"Yeah."

"It was such a good show we let it go on. Didn't shoot. Just watched those dogs draw blood."

"Yeah. So?"

"Well, you corner something, make it afraid, it'll turn mean. Crazy mean. Has to. That's how it was with that bear. Just went wild wanting to hit something, anything, anybody, to give back some pain."

"What happened?"

"He got one dog before we shot him. Hit that dog so hard, it flew. I swear that dog was dead, all busted up inside, before it hit the ground."

I nodded. Riley wasn't talking about bears and hunting dogs. He was talking about the soldiers. Between the Government keeping them here and us drawing blood at every turn, they were cornered. Cosgrove's little traps would just make it worse. I thought of a soldier camp we had shot up a couple nights before. After the soldiers quit spraying the darkness with bullets, one of them started screaming at us, calling us fucking cowards and every other dirty name, daring us to come out and fight. The soldier sounded like he had gone crazy. At the time, I thought it was funny. Now, I wasn't so sure.

"So what you reckon they'll do?" I said.

"Don't know." He looked down at the ground and shrugged.

"Why don't you tell Jane about this?"

He looked up and smiled. "No. Jane don't listen. Not when she's got her mind set. You know how she is."

I nodded. I knew.

It was maybe a week later that we found the boy. He was terrified, and we had trouble understanding him at first. Then we didn't want to believe what he said.

He had hid in the woods when the soldiers came. The soldiers had surrounded the village, driven everyone out of the houses. Then he ran as fast as he could to find help.

The boy didn't have to lead us there. The smoke from a burning house showed us the way.

We moved in slow, worried about an ambush. There were bodies at middle of the village, next to the well. Some had been shot in the head once. Others had been damn near cut in half by the big machine guns.

We spread out, to see if the soldiers were still there, to find survivors. All the buildings I checked were empty, except the last one.

72

A woman was on the table. Her shredded clothes lay under her, already sodden with the blood from the wide deep cut across her throat. Her eyes were wide open staring at the ceiling. Flies buzzing all around.

I stood there until I felt my stomach coming up. I got outside and bent over but didn't vomit. When I felt under control again, I stood up and found myself facing Jane.

She looked at me for a moment and then began to move toward the house. I stepped in front of her and put my arm across the doorway, blocking her.

She looked at me.

"Don't," I managed to say. There was a terrible taste in my mouth.

She kept looking at me and lightly put one hand on the arm I had across the doorway. I dropped it and let her pass.

When I forced myself to go back in, Jane was covering the woman with a blanket. I felt ashamed that I hadn't done that.

Before she pulled the blanket over the woman's face, Jane stopped and closed the eyes. She started to move the blanket again and hesitated. She took a crumpled piece of paper from the woman's mouth. There was blood was on it. Then Jane pulled the blanket all the way up and went outside. I followed.

She opened the crumpled paper. It was a copy of the sign with Jane's picture. We looked at in silence before Jane folded the paper and put it in a coat pocket.

We walked back toward the well. Now there were a few people standing, looking at the bodies. The survivors. They stood without moving, as still as if the world itself had come to a stop. I could hear the buzzing cloud of flies feasting on the dead, the pop and crackle of the burning house, and the thump of my heart.

Then we heard gunfire, coming from the other side of the village. While the survivors scattered, scrambling for hiding places, Jane and I ran toward the shots. For a few seconds, we heard the heavy rattle of automatic rifles. The rattle stopped, replaced by single rifle shots. Then silence.

Ahead, at the top of a rise, a big man named McGill was dragging a soldier into the road. Riley and a couple of our men followed. When Jane and I got closer, I saw the soldier looked bad. Real bad. He was covered in dirt and blood, and was bleeding from his mouth and cuts on his face. Finally, McGill threw the man on the ground in front of Jane and kicked him in the ribs. Gasping and retching, he curled up in a ball with his hands over his head. He was quivering.

McGill looked all set to keep beating the soldier.

"Stop!" Jane shouted.

McGill's eyes were crazy looking. Had he cut loose again, I don't think anything would've stopped him. But Jane held him.

"Stop," she said. Calm and even. Something in McGill seemed to turn, and he took a step back.

"We found this one, and two others, draining a bottle." Riley said. "He gave up. Other two are dead."

She nodded and looked down at the soldier, still curled up at her feet.

"Sit up," she said. "Sit up. I want to talk with you."

He just lay there shaking, waiting for the next blow.

"We ain't gonna hit you," she said.

It wasn't until Jane got us to step back some that the soldier tried to sit up. He could barely move and had to support himself with trembling arms to keep from falling on his face.

Jane squatted in front of him so he could see her face and she could see his. When he seemed able to focus on her, she took the folded piece of paper out of her pocket and held it up for him to see. His eyes worked back and forth between the drawing and her face. He stiffened, recognizing her.

Folding the paper again, she put it away. Then she turned and looked back in the direction of the heaped bodies. The soldier looked there too.

She turned back to him and said, "Why?"

At first, he didn't react. He just slumped forward, leaning on his arms, swaying a little. Then he glanced around as if calculating his chances of escape. At last, he looked at the ground and said, his voice cracking, "The officer told us. It was him. He made us to do it."

I felt like shouting at him, asking him if the officer made him rape and murder that woman. But I didn't. It wouldn't do any good. I felt sick again, like my stomach would come up.

Jane just looked at him, steady.

"But I didn't do anything," the soldier went on. He was pleading now, desperate, looking around for a trace of pity in our faces. "I didn't do anything!"

Jane said nothing.

"Let's shoot the lying bastard and be done with it," McGill said. "Who wants to do it? I'll be glad to."

The soldier hunched forward, whimpering. All hope gone.

"No," Jane said, her voice almost a whisper. "I'll do it."

I looked at her, unable believe what I had heard.

"I'll do it," she repeated and stood up. Her voice was now firm and even. Almost normal.

All of us, except the soldier, gaped at her. God forgive me. The first thing I felt was relief. I didn't want to pull the trigger. But I couldn't let her do this.

I grabbed her arm and pulled her away from the soldier and the silent men standing around him. After a few steps, she wrenched her arm away, but kept walking with me.

"You crazy?" I said. "Why did you say that?"

"It's my burden."

"No. You don't want to do this."

"If I don't, will you?"

I should have said yes. But I hesitated.

She looked at me. Reading me.

"Let McGill. He wants to."

"No."

"Then we'll draw straws. Cast lots. Let God decide."

"God has decided. I've said it. I have to do it."

"No one should expect this of you."

"They do now."

Then she turned from me and walked back toward the men who were still watching her in silence. I followed.

Jane worked the bolt of her rifle, loading a new cartridge. Her hands were trembling a little. She looked down at the soldier and told him this was his chance to make peace with God, to ask forgiveness for his sins.

The soldier seemed not to hear her. He just rocked back and forth, crying and wailing like an abandoned child.

We all looked at her. She didn't look at us, only at the soldier. Then she lifted her rifle, David Winslow's rifle, and aimed. A long moment. Then she screamed and did it.

Somehow, all the fine details of that instant have been scratched on my memory. I can still see how the men were standing. I can still see the look on Jane's face. And the soldier's.

I know, of course, that I could not have seen all those things at once. But that's how I remember it.

The shot hit the soldier in the forehead. The back of his head blew out, and he snapped backward, one arm flew up with the force of the impact. Then the limp body fell over, blood gushing and spurting out of the head.

We all stood still, waiting until Jane moved again. She worked the bolt of her rifle, ejecting the spent shell and loading a new one. That released us, and we started moving again.

We spent the rest of that long day helping with the dead, digging graves and such. I had long since gotten used to seeing the dead. But burying children . . . that was something else. Maybe there's a way a man can get used to seeing that, but I pray to God I never do.

It was almost dark when we had done what we could and got ready to leave. McGill came over to Jane. He had a face like an old boot, lined and hard. There was just enough light to see he was crying.

"What do we do now?" he said.

Jane stepped closer to him and put a hand on his arm. She looked at him and said nothing. She was not crying.

16

As you came upon them, you always heard a child or two crying with hunger, or sobbing with some grief deeper than words. But the others were silent. They were too hungry and too weary to talk.

At first, here and there, we saw handfuls of our people on the trails and the roads. But soon crowds of people were on the move, plodding toward somewhere they might have kin, or just away. A few had horses and carts for their things. Some had an old wheelbarrow. Most carried what they could in a sack thrown over a shoulder or dragged on the ground. Many had little more than the clothes on their backs.

We couldn't do much for them. We had no food to give them. We had no medicine. Jane talked with them, prayed with them, but then moved on. Riley and I helped how we could, mostly digging graves.

What we had seen in that village happened again, here and there in the mountains close to the big road. Soldiers slaughtered children and old folk, raped women, and burned homes. In a few of the larger towns, or where folks fought back, the soldiers dropped bombs and used artillery.

It was plain what the soldiers were doing. They were trying to drive our people away. The people fed us, hid us, and nursed our wounded. Our people watched for the soldiers and told us what they were doing. We couldn't fight without their help.

The soldiers were going to drain the pond to get the fish. If they had to, they would kill us all. Kill women and children like they were lice. Not a trace of mercy. Until I had seen that village, I would have thought it impossible. I mean, I had read old history books, and those books are full of stories of blood and slaughter. But to me, those stories were always just words on a page about other people in another time. I suppose those folks didn't believe it could happen either, not to them. Now it was happening to us.

I thought about the prisoner Jane had let go. Lieutenant Hobbes. He was the only soldier I had ever heard say more than a few words. I wondered how he would explain this. He had talked about "law and order." What had he said? "Law and order make everything possible." I wanted to tell him that "law and order" had made the slaughter of my people possible. I wondered if he had known about all this back when we had him. Maybe his army had done this before. Maybe not. Hobbes said he had seen things as a boy, terrible things, things we couldn't imagine. Maybe he had. I just wanted show him what he had done to us for a stretch of road.

What had happened, what could still happen, lay heavy on all of us. But for Jane it was worse. She had told us God wanted us to fight, and if we fought, God would bring us victory. But for all our fighting, killing, and dying, the Government's army kept coming. More soldiers, more weapons, and more supplies kept arriving. We were neither winning nor losing. So in the end, we would lose. If Jane had been wrong, all the blood and suffering was for nothing. This burden was on her from the start, of course, but back then, she could still smile, still laugh. She had come a long way since then. We all had. The path didn't seem to lead where God had promised.

Then one day, Jane put her finger on the map and said, "There."

She was pointing to Canton. It was the first big town the Government soldiers had taken when they had rolled out of Asheville. It was east of us, a five or six day walk, and beyond where any of our units operated.

Riley and I waited, hoping she would explain.

She said nothing.

"The Spirit?" Riley said.

She nodded.

It was a hard trip. We had bad luck with the weather. But there was more to it than that.

On the second or third day, I can't remember which, it rained all day and into the night. We camped in an abandoned cabin and built a fire in the old stone hearth. All three of us sat, crowding the flames, trying to get warm and dry. Sitting there, I could look at Riley and Jane. I watched their faces in the firelight. As the heat worked its way into him, Riley's face relaxed, and he closed his eyes. He fell asleep and from the little smile that came and went on his lips,

Jane just looked into the fire, her face blank, her mind somewhere else. I was looking at her when she glanced up at me. But I didn't look away, embarrassed, as I once had.

She smiled. But her eyes didn't smile.

"Fire feels good," she said.

"Yeah," I said. "Getting dry?"

She nodded. "You?"

I nodded. "I'll add some wood before long."

She looked back into the fire and went back to wherever she had been. I wanted her to tell me what she was thinking. I wanted to know why we were going to Canton. I wanted to help. But I let the moment pass.

We walked east in a steady rain all the next day. To make better time, we ran the risk of using roads. People trying to get away from the soldiers were moving west, the opposite direction, on the same road. As we passed them, most gave us no more than a glance. They were too miserable to take much notice of three wet travelers going the wrong way.

Just before sunset, the rain quit, and we passed a small bunch of folks who had camped on the roadside. They had a few wagons and some cook fires going. The smell of their food made me hungry, but I knew we couldn't stop. So I paid them no mind until we heard a voice behind us calling, "Janie! That you? Janie?"

I wheeled around and saw a boy, maybe fifteen years old, running toward us, splashing through puddles on the road. He was grinning and shouting, "Janie! It's you! It's you!" When he got to Jane, they wrapped their arms around one another.

I looked at Riley. He had one eyebrow raised, the way he always did when he found something interesting.

"Is everyone . . . OK?" she said.

"Yeah," he said, a big grin on his face. "We got out before any soldiers came around. We're all here. Come on."

Jane, remembering Riley and me, told us this was Ricky, her little brother. He was so happy to see her that it was hard not to smile along with him.

Jane was grinning too until Ricky said, "Papa didn't believe it. He said you couldn't be here. Just wait till he sees you."

We went back along the road to the little camp. Jane's family had a wagon with a rain cover rigged on one side. They had a good fire going with a cooking pot hanging over it.

As we approached, a man and a woman sitting by the fire stood up. The man had only one arm. The other had been cut off above the elbow. He had to be Jane's father, but his face was blank and hard. Angry.

The woman, Jane's mother, looked surprised, putting both hands to her face. She glanced at the man for a moment before letting herself smile. Then she came out and embraced Jane real tight, whispering something in her ear.

Finally, the woman drew Jane over to the fire. The man just continued to stand there, still and silent as an old tree.

"Hello, Papa," she said.

"Janie."

"How you been?"

He gave a little shrug. "You?"

"Good."

Without taking his eyes off Jane, he gave a little jerk of his head toward where Riley and I were standing. Jane told him our names.

The man did not even look at us. It wasn't hard to tell he wished we weren't there.

Jane's mother had us all sit down, and her father said a prayer. Then we ate. It was the first warm food I had eaten in a while. But Jane's father never said another word. Her mother and brother kept glancing at him as they talked about how they had packed up and left, how bad the weather been, what was happening to this relative or that neighbor, and such things. They didn't ask Jane anything about Winslow or the war. They didn't even ask why she was walking east when everyone else was going west.

As soon as we finished, Riley and I thanked them for the meal and excused ourselves. We needed to find a place to bed down. There were a few other folks camped here and there, their small fires flickering in the darkness.

We heard a voice call out of the darkness, "You boys are welcome at my fire."

I looked over and saw a man toss some wood on his fire. He waved to us. Something about him was familiar. We went over to the man.

When I got closer, I recognized him and said, "We met you a while back. With Jane."

"That's right," he said and put out his hand. "John Darcy."

We shook his hand and gave our names. He invited us to have a seat. Then he sat down on a log, but with considerable effort. He laughed and said, "Old age has its blessings, but comfort ain't one of them." Riley and I smiled and sat close to the fire.

Uncle John said, "You know, back at that camp I didn't want to send her off with strangers, but she was so determined to go. I want to thank you for taking care of Janie."

I thought of Jane running down that slope to the wounded man on the road, bullets kicking up dirt all around her. But I said, "You're welcome, but for the most part we just try to keep up with her."

"Well, Janie was always like that," Uncle John said, "always in front. Stubborn about it."

"You're her uncle?" Riley said.

"Her Papa's older brother. But he won't talk to me no more."

"Because of Jane?" I said.

"Yeah. He was angry when I believed in Janie. But when I helped her leave home that just tore it. We ain't spoke since."

"Sorry to hear that," I said.

"We just had dinner over there," Riley said. "The whole time, he barely said a word to Jane."

Uncle John nodded and said, "Now, I don't want you boys to think he's a bad man. He ain't. He's not some whiskey drinker with a mean streak. He's just reached his limit. You saw his arm? Lost that in the militia when he was your age. About five years ago, lost his oldest boy to that winter fever that went through the militia camps."

"Jane never mentioned that," Riley said.

Uncle John continued, "The youngest boy, Ricky, will have to serve soon. And now with this war. . . ." He shook his head. "Anyway, my brother reckons they've given enough. He told her not to go . . ." He shrugged.

Riley and I exchanged a glance. We both knew what Jane did when she was told not to do something.

"Believing in Jane is a hard thing," Uncle John said. "Especially for the folks who knew her before . . . before all this. But that's to be expected. Matthew 13:57, 'And they were offended in him. But Jesus said unto them, A prophet is not without honor, save in his own country, and in his own house.' So it was for our Lord, so it is for Janie."

"Yeah, I see what you mean," I said.

We just sat there, quiet, letting the fire warm us and dry our clothes. After a while, Riley said he was going to find a spot to bed down for the night. "You coming?" he said to me.

"Not yet."

Riley thanked Uncle John for the hospitality, said goodnight, and went off in the darkness.

I said, "I reckon you want to talk to Jane. Should I tell her you're here?"

"No need," he said. "She'll find out and be over directly."

We were quiet again for a while.

"Son," he said, "can I ask you a question?"

"Sure."

"Are you a Christian? Saved and all?"

"I am," I said, remembering the man was a minister.

"Do you believe God sent Janie?"

I paused, considering what to say. "I'm not sure about that, Sir. But I believe she believes it with all her heart. And I believe in her."

"I'm sure she can count on you."

I felt like crying, but held it back. "I won't let her down."

"Good," he said. "I worry about Janie. She knew God had called her long before she was able to tell any of us. Looking back, I can she how she kept herself away from what most girls do. Lonely."

I said nothing.

"I wonder if she'll ever get to have the ordinary joys of life, marriage, raising a family, and all. But Janie has a calling from God, and such folks often don't have ordinary lives."

"You're right, but maybe when the war is over."

"Maybe," he said. "But I wonder if a calling from God, her kind anyways, is ever over."

I said nothing and hoped he couldn't tell what was on my mind. But he could.

He put a hand on my shoulder. "It's hard for a man not to think about what he thinks about. But don't be worrying on the future. I know what it's like in the militia. That's how I got this bad leg. The only future you got is right now. Best keep your mind on that."

"Reckon so," I said. And I knew he was right, but doubted it would make any difference.

I was thinking about this, staring into the fire when Uncle John stood up. Jane came out of the darkness and walked into his open arms. Neither said a word. They hugged, and he patted her back as if trying to soothe her.

She said, "I need to visit with Uncle John a while." Her cheeks were shiny with tears. This surprised me. I had never seen her cry.

I nodded, thanked Uncle John, and left. When I was sure they couldn't see me anymore, I stood in the darkness and watched them. They were sitting side by side. She was talking, but I couldn't make out what she said. He was nodding, listening hard.

Her cheeks were still shiny with tears, but she also looked happy.

I found Riley and laid out my bedroll. He was still awake, and we talked for a while about Jane's family, especially the way her father treated her.

"I just don't understand that," I said. "Don't understand that at all."

"There's no figuring kin," Riley said. "Hard to understand your own. Damn near impossible to understand anybody else's."

In the middle of the night, I woke up. Someone was standing over us holding a lantern. It was Jane's father.

"Mr. Darcy?" I said. "What's wrong?"

He did not say anything at first. Then he swallowed hard and said, "Got something to say to you boys." I woke Riley.

"I reckon I need to thank you for taking care of my little girl," Mr. Darcy said.

Riley and I nodded.

"I sure would like to see her come home for good. Safe." He looked close to tears. Then he walked away.

We were quiet for a while until Riley spoke.

"Like I said. No figuring kin."

17

Just as we reached the door, someone on the other side pulled it open. There was just enough light to see a man with a pistol, aimed at us.

We froze. Riley and I were on either side of Jane, holding her up. Her left shoulder was bleeding.

The man said nothing, and we didn't move.

"Please," Jane said.

He motioned us inside and closed the door behind us.

"Come back here," he said.

We carried Jane down a hallway to another room. The man pulled on one side of a tall set of bookshelves. It swung open like a door on hinges to reveal a chamber about three feet deep, four wide, and six high. He motioned for us to go in.

The man gave us pieces of cloth for bandages and a blanket. He almost had the door closed when he said, "What's your name girl?"

"Jane," she said. "Thank you."

"Thank me later, Jane. If this door starts to open, and I haven't called you by name, it'll be soldiers. Start shooting."

He closed the door. Darkness. The fading sound of his steps.

We stuck the cloth under Jane's coat where she was bleeding and draped the blanket over her. I used one hand to put pressure on the wound and held my rifle with the other. I heard the sounds of Riley checking his rifle. Once our breathing slowed down, there was complete silence.

Standing in the dark, I couldn't quite believe this was happening. After a week of hard travel, we had reached the edge of Canton at twilight. From a hill, we still could see the whole town and the camp full of soldiers. Jane was all set just to walk straight into town as soon as it got dark. But I balked.

"This don't make any sense. What are we doing here?" I said, determined not to go anywhere until she gave me a straight answer.

"Have faith," she said.

"We do," I said, "but--"

Riley interrupted. "If you'd tell us what we're supposed to do, then we can do it."

She frowned, seeming to consider this. "I'm looking for someone," she said.

"Someone?" I said.

"Or something."

"Something?" Riley said.

She nodded, and for a moment, I thought it was all she would tell us. But she added, "There's someone in that town, someone who knows something, something that will make the difference."

"You shouldn't go," I said. "Tell us what to look for."

"I can't. The Spirit has to lead me."

"There's hundreds of soldiers and only three of us," I said. "We're alone. This is too dangerous."

She paused a long time before taking a folded piece of paper from inside her coat. Then she held it out to me. "Remember this?"

I remembered. It was the paper from the mouth of the dead woman. The woman's dried blood was on it. I didn't want to touch it, but couldn't help staring at it. The memory of that day made me feel sick.

"Take it," she said. "Take it." There was a hardness in her voice that surprised me. I obeyed. But I didn't open it.

She pointed at the paper and said, "I'll do whatever it takes to stop the soldiers. Whatever it takes."

I looked up from the paper into her eyes.

"Will you?" she said.

The question made me angry. After all this time, and all we had been through, how could she ask me that? But I didn't say anything. I just nodded.

Then she took the paper from my hand.

Once it got good and dark, we worked our way into town along overgrown back streets, past abandoned houses collapsing with neglect. Here and there, you could see a house still in use, a lamp glowing in the window. Jane didn't go toward the center of town—where the most soldiers were bound to be. I was beginning to hope we wouldn't run into any trouble, when we turned a corner and saw two soldiers walking toward us. For a second, they were surprised and stopped. Then one shouted, "Hey!"

We turned and ran back the way we had come. Just before we got around the corner, one of the soldiers fired a burst at us. Jane screamed.

But she managed to stagger around the corner before going down.

Riley went to Jane, and I took cover at the corner of the building. I fired a few wild shots at the soldiers, trying to keep them back. Then I heard Riley shout, "Let's go!" I turned, expecting to see Jane dead, expecting it all to be over, expecting the world to slam to a halt. But she was moving, grimacing. She had one hand on a shoulder, blood showing between her fingers. In the other hand, she still held her rifle.

The world kept turning.

There was no time for anything but getting away. Riley grabbed Jane, got her on her feet, and dragged her toward an alley between two buildings to our left. I followed, looking behind us for the soldiers.

We reached the end of the alley, turned a corner, crossed a street, and went down another alley. As we got to another street, we heard the sound of a government truck, tires squealing to a stop. Then the shouts of many soldiers. Close.

Riley whispered, "We gotta hide."

We headed for some houses. Riley led her toward the nearest one, but Jane said, "No. There." She pointed to the next. I couldn't see why, but there was no time to argue.

Now we were hiding inside that house, in the dark, listening. After a few minutes, we heard heavy footsteps. Soldiers. I took my hand off Jane's shoulder to have two for my rifle. I felt her move. Her rifle had come up toward the door.

The footsteps were almost right in front of us. The floorboards creaked. A short murmur of voices, and then the footsteps went away.

We waited in the dark silence. I put one hand back on Jane's bandage. Then we heard footsteps again. One set. Moving slow.

"Jane?" a voice said. "Jane, it's safe. Do you hear me? Jane?"

"Yes, I hear you," she said. "It's safe."

"I'm going to open the door now."

I felt the door move, saw dim lamp light, and felt the fresher air.

Riley went out first, weapon ready. After a moment, he said, "Come on out."

We got Jane into a chair. She looked pale and sweaty, but she smiled at us. Her eyes smiled too.

The man turned up the lamp. He looked old and tired.

"Welcome to my home," he said.

When I woke up the next morning, light showed around a heavy covering on the windows. I guessed Riley was out in the front room, still on watch. I was propped up against the wall. Jane lay on a pallet. She was looking at me.

"Hey," I said, "How are you?"

"Good," she said. "You?" Her voice sounded weak.

"Better than last night. We should change that dressing."

She had been lucky with the wound. The bullet had passed straight through, missing bone. With rest, food, and clean bandages, I hoped she would be fine.

She seemed to be waiting for something.

So I went ahead and said, "I told you this was too dangerous."

She just looked at me in that way of hers.

"Don't give me that look, Jane," I said. "You were almost killed last night, killed for nothing. You shouldn't take risks like this."

"You need to understand, my life is in God's hands," she said. "If He wants my life, He will take it. If He has work for me, He will protect me. He did last night."

"Just barely. Doesn't the Bible say, 'Thou shalt not tempt the Lord thy God?' I thought that meant 'Don't take stupid chances and expect God to save you.'"

"Why shouldn't I risk my life? You risk yours. So does Riley. Every man in our militia risks his life."

"It's different."

"Why? Cause I'm a girl?"

"No, because you're important. I'm not. I'm just one more rifle. But if we lose you . . ."

It was a good argument, but it wasn't my real reason. I wanted to protect her.

"I understand," she said, "but God has a plan."

Just then, the man walked in with plates of food.

"I thought you'd be hungry," he said.

Jane thanked him and said that she was very hungry. The man and I helped her sit up so she could eat. As we ate, she asked about him.

He sat in a chair. His name was Carl Degler. Just before the Plague, he, his wife, and daughter had moved to Canton and rented this house.

"Good deal," Carl said, "only paid one month of rent for 26 years." They had come through the Plague and the bad times that followed. But both his wife and his daughter were now dead. Sickness. Carl was alone.

"How did you survive all these years?" Jane said.

"I have tools. I can fix or build most anything. I dug wells. Repaired roofs. Sharpened knives. Traded work for food. That and our vegetable garden got us through. Just barely sometimes, but with God's help, we always did."

"But what did you do before the Plague?"

"I was in construction. Roads mostly. My specialty was using explosives."

"Explosives?" Jane said, leaning forward.

"Take it easy there," said Carl. "You don't want to open that wound again. Now that I think of it, we should change that bandage." He started out to fetch a clean cloth.

"No!" Jane said. "Tell me about what you did with explosives."

Carl hesitated, puzzled by Jane's excitement. "Well, to build a road you sometimes have to move a lot of rock and earth. So you set off a small charge and then it's easier to--"

"Could you destroy a road or bridge?"

Carl still did not see what she was thinking, but I did.

"Yeah," said Carl. "When I was young, I learned how to do that in the Army."

"Could you still do that?"

"Well, I suppose. But those explosives don't exist anymore."

"How about what's in the Government's bombs?"

He was quiet for a moment.

"We'd best change that bandage," he said and left the room.

We waited in silence for him to come back.

He knelt next to Jane and began to remove the old dressing.

"Last night," he said, "I was going to turn you away. I didn't want trouble."

"Why'd you help us?" Jane said.

"Because my wife would've helped you. Because you said please. Maybe I was just tired of being alone and afraid."

"God brought me to your door, Carl. I was sent here to find someone. You."

He was still for a long moment, looking at her. I couldn't tell if he believed her or not. Then he nodded and started in on the dressing again.

When we were done, he stood up slowly.

"I'm too old to fight," he said, "but I can teach someone smart, someone who has steady nerves. Do you have someone like that?"

"We do," Jane said. "We have many."

"Can you get the things I need? They'll be difficult to find. Maybe impossible."

"We will. We'll find a way."

"All right then," he said as though he had just agreed to fix a roof or dig a well. "I'd better get some food for your other man." He went out.

Jane looked at me, waiting for me to say something. But I said nothing. I got up and went to the front room. It was my turn to be on watch.

She wanted to leave that night. Riley and I refused. She needed to heal up before traveling. But she wouldn't listen.

"Go on then," Riley said. "Stand up."

Grimacing with the effort, she got to her feet. Putting one hand against the wall, she said, "Don't worry about me. We should leave at dark. Carl's the key. We need to get him to Winslow."

Riley and I exchanged a look.

"Then take your hand off the wall," he said.

She glared at him and took her hand down. For a moment, she managed to stand. Then her knees buckled, and she sat down, her back against the wall.

Standing up had taken a lot out of her. Her voice wasn't much more than a whisper. "Get Carl to Winslow. Don't waste time."

"And we just leave you here?" I said.

"Yes," she said, her voice louder.

"Don't talk nonsense," Riley said. "We ain't leaving you."

The next few days were strange. It was dangerous to be in that house. Dangerous for us. Dangerous for Carl. Several times we had to hide behind the bookcase because soldiers were nearby. They didn't come into the house, but Carl said you could never tell when they might. Other than that, it was quiet--the quietest time we had had since the war had begun. Riley and I took turns keeping watch and sitting with Jane. And Carl fed us real well, emptying his pantry.

"Eat up boys," he said. "Don't let it to go to waste."

Carl knew he was leaving that house for good. He spent hours going through his possessions, deciding what to bring. Mostly, he had tools. But he said he only needed a few of them for working with explosives. The rest, a room full of fine saws, wrenches, hammers, and such, he would have to leave. And then there were personal things—pictures of his family, letters, and other keepsakes. He couldn't bring much. The rest, like the tools, had to be left behind.

It was strange that he would just up and go off with strangers. While he was cleaning up after supper, I asked him about that.

"Yeah," he said, "don't make much sense. Sitting around here, waiting to die alone, makes even less."

"But why get mixed up in our fight?" I said. "I mean, the Government's not doing anything to you, is it?"

"No. Not yet. They'll even make some things better around here. It used to be pretty dangerous around here. That's why I built that hiding place. It was for my wife and daughter in case anyone got in the house when I wasn't here. Now the soldiers have run off the thieves and other scum that used to hang about. Because the Army is here, the local traders already have food I haven't seen since before the Plague. And someday, the Government might bring back indoor plumbing and electricity. Telephones. Maybe even radio."

"So if the Government's doing all that, why fight them?"

"This Government ain't like the old one. Sure, the old Government sometimes pushed people around, but you could say whatever you damn well thought about it, and about the folks who ran things. It was supposed to work for us, and we could raise hell when it didn't. Plenty of folks did."

"And this Government?"

"From what I've seen, do what you're told, you'll be fine. But get in the way, you're nothing. They want us to be afraid. Everything comes down to pointing a gun."

I told Carl about what the Government was doing to our people, about what I had seen in that village. I didn't tell him about the woman on the table, or the soldier Jane had shot. I didn't tell him, but I couldn't help remembering those things.

"You saw this with your own eyes?" he said. "It wasn't something you just heard about, a friend-heard-it-from-a-friend kind of thing, was it?"

"I wish I hadn't. But I did. With my own eyes."

He sat down in a chair, folded his arms across his chest, and said, "Then I'm doing the right thing. Maybe the best thing I've ever done."

18

"Damn," Carl said. "That girl's gonna kill herself."

Jane was up ahead, leaning against a tree, winded from the last climb. I went to her, put a hand on her shoulder, and said, "Don't make yourself sick. Sit down. Have some water."

She turned, knocking my hand away.

"No!" she shouted. Her eyes seemed hard, crazy. For a moment, I was surprised. Then I got angry. But I knew better than to say anything. Since leaving Canton, Jane had pushed us to go faster, to get to Winslow sooner. She had gotten it in her head there wasn't a moment to lose, and nothing would change that.

"Come on. Come on. Let's go," she would say, and wave us forward, like we were little boys dawdling at our chores. I was tired of this, tired of being pushed around, tired of her.

She started up the trail again. Slowly. Each step a heaving act of will.

Riley and Carl came up and stood next to me. The three of us just watched her.

She stopped, turned, and saw us standing there.

"Come on. Come on. Let's go," she shouted, waving us forward.

Going up the last hill to Central Camp, I thought she wouldn't make it. But she walked into camp on her own, head up, back straight, and carrying her own rifle—putting on a real show. When our men saw her, they cleared a path for her.

She wanted to see Winslow right away, but she was told he wasn't around. Campbell was. While someone ran to fetch him, she stood quietly, holding her rifle in the crook of her arm, just as she had when I first saw her. She swayed a little, and a trickle of sweat came down the side of her face. The muscles in her jaw were bunched tight. I expected her to collapse any moment.

Finally, the men around us made way for someone.

"Jane, you're alive," Campbell said. He didn't look happy or unhappy. He didn't even look surprised.

"Yes," she said and turned to look at Carl. Just then her eyelids fluttered and closed, and her knees buckled. Riley and I caught her and let her down to the ground. Campbell knelt by her. Her eyes opened, and she reached up and grabbed him by the shirt. Then she passed out.

We carried Jane to a shed where the wounded were tended. An older man named Simpson was in charge. He was taking off her coat to look at her shoulder, when her eyes opened a little, and she said in a weak voice, "Papa? Papa?" Then she was out again. Simpson pulled away the bandage and looked at the wound.

"She gonna be OK?" Riley said.

"Don't look infected," Simpson said. "But she must be all wore out from losing blood. We'll have to wait and see."

Campbell took Riley, Carl, and me outside and said, "What the hell's going on?"

We explained. Carl did most of the talking. Campbell just stood there listening to him, nodding now and then, but not saying anything. When Carl finished, Campbell still didn't say anything. Instead, he looked like he was thinking real hard and ran his fingers through his hair several times.

"Follow me," he said.

We walked for a bit until we reached a wagon covered by a heavy canvas tarp. Campbell had Riley pull back the tarp, and he climbed up amid the crates. After poking around for a minute, he pulled out something shaped like a brick, but wrapped in dark green paper. Tossing it to Carl, he said, "Can you use this?"

Carl caught it and turned it over in hands and peeled back some of the paper. It looked like clay. Carl touched and sniffed it.

"You're damn right I can use it," he said. "This is a plastic explosive, C-4 or something like it. What else you got?"

"Take a look," Campbell said.

Riley and I boosted Carl up into the wagon, and he began looking through the crates.

Campbell climbed down and gestured for us to follow him. We walked about ten yards, and he said to us, "Can we trust him?" He kept his voice low so Carl couldn't hear us.

"I think so." I told you how we found him, how he hid us from the soldiers, and left everything to come here.

"But why would a man do that?" he said.

"Jane," Riley said.

"She can have that effect on some," Campbell said, laughing.

I almost said, "But not on you?" I had no business asking a Colonel such questions and was glad I held my tongue.

Just then Carl started calling for us to come back. He was excited about something he had found in the wagon. We all started that way, but Campbell told us that he would see to Carl. He said our job was to take care of Jane.

So Riley and I turned and started walking to the shed where Jane was resting.

"Let's see," I said, "since we've been taking care of her, Jane's been shot at, wounded, almost captured, and now she's near walked herself to death."

"Well," Riley said, scratching his beard, "I think we've done a damn fine job. Considering."

Jane came to on the second day. She looked up, blinking slowly at Riley and me. Her first words were, "Where's Carl?"

"We're just fine," Riley said. "Thanks for asking."

"Where's Carl?" she said.

"He's with Campbell," I said.

"Good," she said and closed her eyes.

I started to tell her more, about the bricks of explosives, and how excited Carl had been, but she was already asleep, a little smile on her face.

The next day, Jane was awake, sitting on her bed and leaning against the wall of the cabin, when Campbell came to see her. There were dark circles under her eyes, and she was pale.

"How are you Jane?" he said.

"Tell me. What's happened?" she said.

Campbell stood on one side of Jane's bed. Riley and I on the other.

"The soldiers hold the road all the way to the tunnel at Snowbird Mountain," he said. "We hit them, but they just keep coming. More men. More trucks."

He paused like he didn't want to tell us.

"Tell me," she said.

"Massacres. At least two. Maybe more. We don't know for sure."

"Damn!" Riley said.

"Riley," Jane said, real gentle. "Don't curse. Please."

"Sorry," he said, looking down. "Couldn't help it."

None of us said anything. For a moment, I was back in that house, smelling the woman's blood, hearing the flies.

"What about Carl?" Jane said.

Campbell nodded. "He says we can collapse sections of the road and make landslides big enough to block it. But we need to get more explosives. A lot more."

"How?" Jane said.

"We got this batch from soldiers. Some will trade equipment, ammo, you name it, for whiskey, for gold and jewelry. But that's a tricky business. It might take some time."

"How much time?" she said.

Campbell shrugged. "Could be weeks. But if we don't get it trading, we'll have to find a way to take some. And that could be . . . hard."

"Is Carl here?" Jane said. "I want to talk with him."

"He's with some our men scouting the big road for the best places to attack. He'll be away a few more days."

"What about Winslow?" Jane said.

"He's someplace where the soldiers won't find him. Do you need to send a message to him?"

Jane just shook her head.

Campbell said goodbye and was turning to go when I said, "Hey, Colonel," He stopped and looked at me.

"Until all this happens," I said, "what're we supposed to do?"

"Wait."

So we waited. Riley and I sat with her and fed her. At least once a day, Simpson checked her wound, which was healing fast, and changed the dressing. The circles under her eyes went away, and she got her color back.

Every morning, she would wake early and pray for an hour or more. She did the same at night. Once she started feeling a little better, she would get dressed and walk around camp, carrying her rifle. Each day she walked a little more and seemed stronger. She always spent some time talking and praying with the wounded. Campbell came by now and then. He didn't have much to say. He was still waiting for news.

Jane rested, but she seldom appeared relaxed, except when Riley got her laughing with one of his funny stories. Jane and I didn't say much when I sat with her. I felt a kind of wall between us, a wall that hadn't been there before going to Canton.

Instead of talking, I read to her. I had borrowed a Bible from someone in camp. Though she couldn't read, she knew many of the stories from listening in church and asked me to read certain one. Stories with fighting and wars were her favorites. In those stories, the Jews were always in terrible trouble, getting conquered and enslaved by their enemies. But God would not abandon His people and He would raise up a Judge or a Prophet to lead the people to a great victory.

One night she asked to hear the story of the Prophetess Deborah in the Book of Judges. I read the story and came to the last verse, "So let all thine enemies perish O LORD: but let them that love him be as the sun when he goeth forth in his might. And the land had rest forty years."

When I finished, I looked up. Jane seemed happy, lost in the story's promise of victory and peace. I watched her for a long moment until she turned to me and smiled.

"Jane," I said. "You believe we're just like the folks in those stories, don't you? God delivered them and He'll deliver us."

"Don't you?" she said. Jane had a way of turning things around. I had asked her a question, but ended up trying to explain myself.

"Well, I don't know," I said. "They're God's chosen people. That's why He worked miracles for them. But we're just people. God wants us to have faith, to be good, to go to heaven, and all, but I don't know if He's fighting the Government for us."

"Then why are those stories in the Bible?"

I stared at her. I had no idea what she was talking about.

"God put all those stories about war in the Old Testament," she said, "didn't He?"

"Yeah, of course."

"So, what's He trying to tell us?"

"Up home, our minister said the whole Old Testament showed how God worked to bring forth Christ and His salvation to the world. It shows how much God loves us."

"That's true. But the Bible also shows us how to be God's people. In peace and war. In good times and bad."

"But we're not like those people in the Bible. They were called to great things . . . I mean--"

"And we aren't important to God? Just backward hillbilly trash? Is that it?"

"Well . . ."

"Compared to Egypt and Babylon and Rome, the Jews weren't powerful or important. And think about how it must've been for people back then. They didn't know they was in the Bible. They was just living their lives, like we are. Put yourself in their shoes."

"I think they wore sandals. Not shoes."

"Oh, be serious," she said, punching me on the arm.

"So we're just like the folks in the Bible?"

"Yes."

"So . . . we're the chosen people?"

"No. Not the chosen people. But I believe . . . . I know God will be with any people who have faith and keep the commandments."

"So . . . God will beat the Government?"

"No. We have to fight. We have to have faith. And God will --"

I said, "'What then shall we say to these things. If God be for us, who can be against us?' Paul to the Romans, Chapter 8."

"Yes," she said, nodding and smiling. "That's it."

"But . . ."

"But what?"

"We've been fighting for months, and the soldiers just keep coming.

And what they are doing to our people . . . How can--"

She cut me off. "How can God let that happen?"

I nodded.

"I don't know. But I do know God is with us. Without God's help, the soldiers would've already beaten us. Think of all the times we've seen God's hand at work."

I nodded. I had seen Jane do amazing things. So part of me was willing to say that God was behind it all. But another part of me wondered if Jane had just had an incredible run of luck. I didn't know much more about luck than the next man. Nobody can tell you where luck comes from, how to keep it, or how to get it back. But I knew, knew for a fact, one thing about luck. Sooner or later, it runs out. Always.

I had to be there when her luck ran out.

"And now God has given us a way to win," Jane said. "Carl."

"Win? Maybe he can stop them for a while. But remember, the Government wants everything, from ocean to ocean. They'll be back. We'll have to keep fighting."

"Of course, we'll have to fight on. The war against Evil goes on till Judgment Day. You know that."

"Yeah, I suppose."

We sat for a while. Silent. I could feel her watching me.

"Do you remember the story where Jesus was sleeping in the boat and a storm came?"

I nodded.

"Do you remember what Jesus said to them? He said, 'Why are ye so fearful? How is it ye have no faith?'"

"I do. I have faith," I said, but I looked away.

"You're a good man," she said. "You do God's will even though you don't understand. I pray for you. I pray you find your way."

"Thank you," I said, forcing myself to look at her.

"I'm tired now. Before you go, could you read a Scripture for me?"

I nodded and picked up the Bible. "What did you want to hear?"

"It's in Romans, after what you said before. It begins, 'Who shall separate us . . .' Know the verse I mean?"

I turned to it and read, "Who shall separate us from the love of Christ? Shall tribulation, or distress, or persecution, or famine, or nakedness, or peril, or sword?"

I stopped, thinking that was what she had wanted to hear. But she told me to keep going. So I read, "As it is written, For thy sake we are killed all the day long; we are accounted as sheep for the slaughter."

I stopped again and looked at Jane. I understood then I wasn't reading this to her. She was reading it to me. Sheep for the slaughter, I thought. Killed all the day long.

I closed the Bible.

"Much obliged," she said.

I nodded, stood up, and turned to go. But at the door, I turned back and told her it was a shame that she couldn't read the Bible herself. I offered to teach her how.

"Once all this is over," I said, "you can learn. It won't take any time at all."

She didn't say anything. So I wondered if I had offended her by being too proud of my schooling.

"I only know how to read because there was a school up home," I said. "I'm not trying to show off or anything."

"I know. You just want to help. But we ought not count on anything after this is over."

She was talking about more than reading. Her Uncle John had told me the same thing.

"I understand," I said. "I'll let you rest now."

She wished me a good night. I went outside and looked up at the sky. It was cloudy, and I couldn't see any stars.

I had spent every waking moment for months with Jane. I had listened to her, followed her, and believed in her. I had risked my life for her, and she had saved mine. I grieved for the things she had to see and do. I knew it to be rank foolishness, but still I had little daydreams about a future with her, not with Maggie. Sometimes I thought I understood Jane. Other times, she was as much a mystery to me as the very first time I saw her walk out of the darkness.

I stood in the dark feeling confused and angry. And lost.

Looking up at the sky again, I saw a small gap had opened in the clouds. For a moment, I could see one bright star.

Then the star disappeared behind the clouds.

19

The fire kept getting bigger. After the first fuel truck had erupted into flames, the ones on either side went. Then every few seconds something new exploded, expanding and feeding the fire. It had been a quiet night, the first chill of fall in the air. Now there was only glaring light and a roar that filled your chest. It was as though Hell had broken through the crust of the earth and was free to rage.

It was our doing. We had set Hell free.

And it was Jane's idea.

We had ambushed a convoy of trucks on its way to a big camp north of Waynesville, where the soldiers kept their trucks and supplies. We pulled down a tree, blocking the road. When the soldiers stopped to move the tree, we started shooting.

But this time we shot at them from only one side of the road. We wanted them all to be looking one way because one of our men was hiding in the brush on the far side. When he was sure he couldn't be seen, he crawled out and put one of Carl's bombs underneath a truck. The bomb had a clock. We hoped it would go off only when the truck reached the camp. When this was done, we pulled back, letting the soldiers think they had run us off. After they had cleared the road, they drove on to Waynesville.

We were miles away on a mountainside, looking out at the town, when the bomb went off. Then other explosions and fires followed. I knew soldiers had to be dying down there, torn apart by explosions, roasted alive and devoured by the flames. That was as terrible a way to die as I could imagine. I told myself they deserved this, and worse. I tried to feel nothing for them. But I knew most of them were not the soldiers who raped and killed. Most dying in the flames just cooked meals, fixed trucks, or handed out supplies. They had been forced into the Government's army, forced to come to our mountains. They probably just wanted to go home.

With each new explosion, each roaring expansion of the fire, I had to force myself not to flinch. But when I looked at Jane, I saw a kind of joy in her face as the Government's tools of war were consumed, as its power to hurt our people was weakened.

It was her triumph. But it was not her only triumph.

Campbell had gotten the explosives, and other things Carl needed, from soldiers trading for whiskey and gold. That had taken almost a month. Carl used the time to teach a handful of men about explosives. A couple times a day, you would hear a loud "Whump!" sound come out of woods, and then the sound of a tree crashing to the ground. That was how Carl had them practice, putting some explosive on a tree and setting it off, shattering the trunk. Then one day Carl and his men were gone. They had gone to strike the big road. And they did it right. Bridges over the Pigeon River and other streams were shattered, collapsing into the water below. In a few places, huge mounds of rock, earth, and trees were knocked from the mountains, blocking the road.

The damage meant the government trucks couldn't come up the road anymore, so a lot of the soldiers went back to their camps. Their airplanes circled overhead looking at what we had done. You could almost feel the whole government army stopped in its tracks, like a bear surprised by a skunk, considering, puzzling about what to do next, and thinking about scuttling backward. That's what we hoped.

This was all Jane's doing. If she hadn't found Carl, nothing would have changed. But Jane wanted to do more than make the soldier stop, or even retreat. She wanted to make them pay for what they had done to us. She said the Spirit had told her that we must attack the Waynesville camp. The bomb was a way to scare the soldiers, to let them know even in their big camps, with fences and machine guns all around, they weren't going to be safe. Not as long as they were near our land. Jane just hoped the bomb would explode, destroying that truck. She didn't expect other explosions. She didn't expect anything to catch fire. She didn't expect it to spread. Not that she told us anyway.

The fire grew until it reached boxes of ammunition, bombs, and shells. The bullets went off like popping corn over a campfire, the tracer rounds going in all directions. Then the bombs and shells started exploding, throwing burning debris high into the air.

"It's like the fireworks Grandpa used to talk about," Riley shouted. "Fireworks for Independence Day."

"This is our Independence Day!" Jane shouted to the men with us. She held David Winslow's rifle above her head, and they cheered.

The cheering died when the flaming debris, spread by a wind, came down on Waynesville. Fires started on roofs and in trees. The wind spread the flames to more buildings. Some debris hit a big church with a tall steeple in the middle of town. The steeple caught fire. A finger of fire pointing at the sky. Then it collapsed, falling onto another building, spreading the fire.

In the time before the Plague, there would have been men to fight such fires. Now, there were none. We could do nothing. The soldiers could do nothing. The fires would just burn. Most houses, of course, had been empty since the Plague. But some people still lived there. Their homes were on fire. Some were dying. And no one would help them.

After a while, the explosions stopped, and the fire settled down to a steady burning, roaring and sending up a vast heaving cloud of black smoke, pushed southward by the wind. The stink of it made me feel sick, and I sat down. I tried to close my eyes and shut it out, but I couldn't. I had to look at it.

I looked until I felt a hand on my shoulder. It was Riley. "Come on," he said.

I nodded and got to my feet. I saw our men had already turned away and were making their way up and over the mountain. Riley, Jane, and I were the last to go.

Jane was still standing, her back to us, looking out at the fire and smoke.

"Jane?" Riley said.

As she turned toward us, I expected to see tears of grief. But she was smiling. She looked at us for a moment and nodded. After one last look toward the fire, she started making her way up the slope toward Riley and me. I stepped in front of her, blocking her path.

"What about those people?" I said. "We just burned their homes. We've taken everything they had. Don't you understand? Winter's coming. Did the Spirit show you how they'll stay warm till spring? Did the Spirit show you what they'll eat? Did the Spirit show you that?"

I didn't realize I had taken a step toward Jane and was shouting at her until Riley put a hand on my shoulder.

I shrugged off his hand.

"God has a plan," she said.

"Plan!? You're saying God did this?"

"God has a plan, and I'm His instrument." Then she just stepped around me and went up the slope. I watched her go. That was all the answer I would get from her.

Riley stood with me for a moment. "Come on," he said and started to follow Jane. But I remained. And watching the smoke boiling up toward heaven, I wondered what else God had planned.

20

It took us three days to get to Campbell, to tell him about Waynesville. Of course, he already knew some of it. News like that travels fast.

Campbell sat with his back against a tree while Jane told him about the ambush, the bomb, the explosions, and the fire. Even then, days later, she was still excited, happy about it. What we had done to those folks in Waynesville still didn't bother her.

Now and then, Campbell would ask a question. Mostly, he just nodded, letting her talk. When she was done, he thanked her and promised to let Winslow know.

She stood up and told him that she was sure the soldiers would leave us alone now.

"Hope you're right," he said. "We'll see."

They looked at one another like traders striking a deal. From the beginning that was how it had been between them. Campbell always had taken her serious. But he had never treated her like someone who had walked off a page of the Bible. Too many of us, me included, had made that mistake.

Jane walked away. Riley got up, stretched, and followed. But after a few steps, he saw I was staying. He stopped and raised one eyebrow in that way he had. I nodded to him. He understood I would explain later.

I turned back to Campbell. He looked more worn down, older and thinner, than I remembered.

"Something on your mind?" he said, putting his head back against the tree.

That's when I told him about wanting to do something else, anything other than following Jane around.

"Why?" he said.

"Rather not say."

"Not good enough. Tell me."

So I told him about Waynesville, about how Jane had been. I didn't say anything about what I was thinking about God. He might understand. He might not. But that was between God and me.

"Fire was an accident," he said. "War's full of accidents."

"That's right, Colonel. We didn't plan on burning out those folks. She just didn't give a damn that it happened. All she could see was what we did to the soldiers."

"So?"

"So that's crazy. And I've had enough of crazy."

"I see," he said. "Does Jane know this?"

"We ain't spoken since Waynesville, and I don't care. If she can't figure it out, let God tell her."

This seemed to amuse him.

"What do you want to do?" he said.

"Anything. Send me to another unit. Put me on guard duty here. Anything."

"How long since you been home?"

I was surprised by the question. "My whole time in the militia. Three years."

"So you've done your three years."

"Just about. But I didn't think that mattered anymore, not with the war and all."

"True enough. If the war goes on, we'll need every man. But we can spare you for a bit. How about a month?"

I was stunned, but I managed to nod. From what I had heard, there hadn't been any trouble near home. It was too far away from the big road for the soldiers to bother. But I didn't know, not for a fact.

Campbell had someone fetch him a pencil and paper. He wrote out a note giving me leave and signed it. He handed it to me and told me to get going. I thanked him and started walking away.

"Now, if the war ends," he said, "no need to hurry back."

If the war ends? I thought.

I explained all this to Riley. He scratched his beard and said, "Well damn, I'd like to go up home. Maybe I oughta get pissed at Jane too."

"Hate to be running out on you," I said.

"Don't matter none."

It did matter, but it was too late to be changing my mind.

We didn't say anything as I packed my things and retied my bedroll. Riley just leaned against a tree, looking down. He said, "Gonna say anything to Jane?"

I shook my head. I had that hollow sick feeling you get when you know,

know for a fact, what you ought to do. But you just won't goddamn do it.

Riley looked like he wanted to talk me out of it, but that wasn't his way.

"Anything I should say to her for you?" he said.

I thought about this. Part of me wanted to say something hard and mean. But I couldn't put that on Riley.

"Tell her to be careful," I said.

Riley laughed. "Oh yeah, that'll do a whole lot of good."

It was time to go. I stuck out my hand. He shook it. We nodded to one another. Then I turned and walked off.

A few minutes later, I was picking my way down a slope through the trees. I heard a noise behind me and turned. It was Jane. She was standing up the slope about twenty yards away looking down at me. Her face didn't give anything away. I just had that hollow feeling again. But I was set on not going to her. Let her come to me.

She raised one hand and held it still. I did the same. Then she turned and headed back uphill. I stood, watching her go. She soon disappeared in the trees. For a little while, I could hear her, the sound fading until all I could hear was a light wind in the trees. Only then did I realize I still had my hand up. Feeling foolish, I put it down and started walking home.

21

It was strange waking up for the first time in my old bed, in the room I had shared with my brother back when we were boys, back when he was alive.

There was a lot of sunlight in the room. That meant my parents had let me sleep well into the morning. I had arrived late the night before, and both of them had stayed up making a fuss over me and feeding me. But I knew they had been up since dawn, working. That was their way. Tomorrow, I would be up at dawn too.

Sitting up and putting my feet on the old wood floor, I looked around. I had been too tired for that last night. The things of my boyhood lay about, dusty and half-forgotten: A collection of rocks and rusting machine parts that I had found. The claw of a black bear my father had killed. My Bible, a dictionary, and a few other books.

Tacked up on the wall was a picture cut from an old magazine. Curling at the edges and fading, the picture showed the Earth, the whole thing, hanging like a blue and white ball in the blackness of space. The picture had been made when my grandfather was young, when men had traveled out to the moon.

I sat there for a while, my feet getting cold, looking at my things. I tried to recall who I had been before the dust had settled on everything. I couldn't do it. Whoever I had been was like a person in a made-up story that I didn't remember well.

I got up and began putting on my clothes. As I buttoned my shirt, I looked across the room at my brother's bed. My mother kept it neater than my brother ever had. Little trace of him remained in the room. I tried to picture him sitting on the edge of the bed, playing that beat-up old harmonica he had found, but I couldn't get his face clear in my mind. I hadn't seen him for a long time, since before I had gone to the militia.

While I was away, he married Maggie, and they moved into a little cabin just up the road. The cabin where he was buried. It would be my cabin when I married her. If I married her.

I would have to visit Maggie. Soon. The thought of it made me nervous. It didn't help, of course, that I had never been with a woman.

I had come close once. Sort of. Well, not really. A few months before I went to the militia, there had been this one time with a girl at Saturday night dance. Even though folks kept an eye on the boys and girls our age, we each managed to slip out into the woods. We kissed, and she rubbed up against me, pressing against my thing until I was near crazy. But then she pushed me away and ran off, laughing, back into the dance. I guess it was a kind of game to her. I couldn't follow, of course, not the way I was sticking out just then. It took me a while to calm down, and by then it was about time to go home. When I saw the girl in church the next morning, she acted like nothing had happened.

So that was my experience with women, with girls anyway. That and the confused daydreaming I had done about this one and that one, including Jane. Of course, I knew what men and women did when they were married. When you grow up on a farm, breeding animals, how babies get made is no great mystery. But knowing what's done is one thing and doing it is another. And doing it with your brother's widow is yet another.

I looked up at the picture I had tacked to the wall and wished I could be that far away from this old world.

The harvest was already in, but there was plenty to do to get ready for winter. Mostly, I chopped and hauled wood. As I worked, I couldn't help thinking about the things I had seen, about Jane and Riley. It was strange not being able to turn to Riley and say what was on my mind. For all I knew, Jane or Riley could be dead now. I thought some about the blue-eyed man too, even though I tried not to. The old dream of him still hadn't come back, but somehow I felt him close by, waiting for me.

My parents only asked about the war in a general way, not what I had done, or about Jane. I'm sure they had heard things and wanted to know. They figured I would talk about all that when I needed to, when I was ready. And if I was never ready, then that was how it would be. It wasn't their way to push me about the past, only the future.

After two days at home, my clothes were clean and patched up nice, and I had made a good pile of firewood. At dinner, my mother asked when I was going to see Maggie. And my brother's grave. I tried to put it off, talking about all the things to be done before the winter. All of that was true enough, but my mother was no fool.

"Nonsense," she said, pushing back from the table and standing up. She looked down at me. "You'll go tomorrow." Then she started clearing the table.

My mother was a reasonable woman. She tended to hear folks out before making up her mind. But when she got that certain tone in her voice, you knew she had drawn a line, and you had best toe it.

It was strange to find myself back in my old seat at the kitchen table, getting scolded. It made me angry. I sat forward and put my fists on the table. "I'm not a boy anymore," I said.

"Then don't act like one," she said, her back to me as she cleared off the dishes into the slop bucket.

This made me even angrier, but the fight went out of me when I looked over at my father. As he loaded up his pipe, he just gave me a wink.

I leaned back in my chair and folded my arms across my chest. The matter was settled. I would go tomorrow.

When Maggie opened the door, she said, "You expecting trouble?"

I was puzzled. Then she pointed to the rifle in my right hand. Carrying it had become as much a habit as wearing my britches. But Maggie wasn't used to such things.

"Sorry," I said, embarrassed.

"Come on then. You can leave it by the door."

I came inside, leaned my rifle against the wall, and took off my hat. She shut the door behind me and then walked across the room to the fireplace. She stood facing the fire with her arms crossed and head down.

I looked around the room. There wasn't much, but it was well kept. Pots and other kitchen things were by the fireplace. A table and chairs sat in the middle of the room. A tall cabinet for clothes stood in a corner next to a back door. A set of shelves on one wall held odds and ends, and a few books. My brother's harmonica sat at the end of one shelf. I wanted to pick it up, but thought better of it. In a corner of the room was the bed. For a moment, I pictured Maggie and my brother, lying there together, naked. It was hard to imagine me in his place.

Not knowing what else to do, I went and stood at the fire with her, a good yard of space between us. I looked into the fire and waited, saying nothing, fumbling nervously with my hat, my heart beating fast. The fire was small and didn't begin to warm the room. I wasn't surprised by that. From what I had seen as I walked up, she didn't have much firewood to spare.

"You'll want to see your brother's grave." She didn't wait for me to answer, but just turned and headed for the back door. She opened the cabinet and pulled out a big coat, which I recognized as my brother's. She put on the coat and went out, leaving the door open for me.

We walked slowly across a field without speaking. Still hard from the first frost of the season, the ground crunched beneath our boots.

I felt strange. I was going to my brother's grave. His death had never been real to me. I had only gotten word of it long after they had put him in the ground. I was going to that grave with his widow, the woman I was supposed to marry, a woman who didn't appear to have much use for me.

And I felt frightened without my rifle.

My brother was buried in the woods beyond the field. It was a nice place, a small clearing a little higher than the surrounding ground. I could see the cabin through the bare branches of the trees and bushes. My parents had told me as he was dying he had asked to be buried there. It would've been easier on Maggie, on me, on everybody if was at the church or on our land. But that's what he had wanted.

His name had been carved into the marker, a heavy piece of plank stuck into the ground. A bed of stones lay atop the grave to keep animals from digging him up. But I knew there was nothing but bones down there now.

I took off my hat and stared at the marker. My brother's face, how he had looked when he smiled and laughed, flickered and jumped in my mind like a candle in a drafty place. I tried to hold the image. Then it was gone. My eyes felt a little wet and I wiped them with the sleeve of my coat.

When I looked up, I saw Maggie was looking right at me, not down at the marker or the stones. Her eyes were dry, clear. Honest.

"Do you want this?" she said.

"Well . . . I don't know," I said. "Do you?"

"If you don't want to try, I'd best head home before winter. And I don't want that."

"Why not?"

She glanced at the marker as if considering whether she would say what was on her mind in its presence. In his presence. She let out a breath and looked at me.

"I don't take much to pity, and that's what waiting for me there. Besides, my folks didn't want me marrying your brother. They didn't think he was . . . steady. And they'll think his dying somehow proves them right. I just don't care to be around that."

"You and my brother chose one another."

She looked back at the marker. "We did."

I didn't bother to ask why. They were both the kind most folks are drawn to, full of life and handsome enough to turn heads. I knew because I wasn't like that at all.

She kept looking at the marker. "He made me laugh. O Lord, how I laughed with him. And you know how he loved music and dancing. That's what I'd thought it would be, laughter and music and dancing. That, and getting in bed and making babies."

When she said this last thing, she looked up at me. Maybe she was trying to see how I would take that kind of talk. Maybe she was just being honest. I felt myself flush, something in me stirring, but still uneasy about feeling that way.

She turned back to the marker. "But it wasn't. Laughter and music don't chop wood, patch the roof, or get a new privy dug. And what's done in bed, well, that don't amount to much if there's no baby."

I didn't say anything.

"I do miss him," she continued. "But every day, I miss him a little less because it was a mistake. If he'd lived, we both would've seen that soon enough."

She turned back to me. "Everyone tells me you're the serious one. The steady one."

"And what if I am? Is that enough? Enough to make you forget?"

"No. There's no forgetting. Not for me. Not for you. But we could try to find something. Something of our own."

"I'll only be here a few weeks."

"I know."

"And when I leave, I might never be back."

She nodded, gave the marker one last glance, and began to walk back to the cabin. I walked by her side. Boots crunching the cold clods.

"You're low on firewood," I said, "If you got an ax, I could chop some."

"I've got one," she said, smiling. "And it's sharp."

I smiled back.

After my chores at home, I would go to Maggie's place and chop wood or do other heavy work until it was near dark. All our talk was practical, about little things, and not like our talk at my brother's grave. On Sunday, we would sit together in church. That was strange because everyone watched us, curious about how we were getting along.

So that's how we began, edging toward one another. Slow and careful. We had stopped being strangers, but we didn't have a word for what we were becoming. Of course, hanging over everything was my leaving. And God only knew what would happen then.

Two days before I was planning to leave, Maggie cooked me a real sit-down dinner. I was so nervous that I could barely taste the food, even though I kept saying it was real good.

I don't think she was as nervous as me, but she didn't say much either. Mostly, she watched me. Maybe she was waiting to see if I was ready for something.

She was standing, cleaning off the plates when she said, "Tell me what happened to you in the militia."

I was so surprised I almost dropped my cup.

"Tell me," she said.

Everything I tried not to think about came up inside me like a rush of vomit. I didn't dare say a word. I would let it all out. And if I did, she would never want me. No one would.

Maggie waited, motionless, still holding a plate.

Looking away, I shook my head. It was all I could manage.

She sat down at the table, laying the plate aside. "You don't have to tell me. Ever. But I want you to know that you can. It's up to you."

"Thank you," I said. And I meant it. I was grateful. But it wasn't because she was willing to listen. That would come later. I was grateful for not having to say anything.

"But there's something else," she said.

"What?"

"Tell me about this girl, Jane Darcy."

"What do you want to know?"

"Folks say God works through her. That true?"

There it was. The question I had never been able to answer.

"Sometimes I thought she was," I said. "Other times I had to wonder about her. Or about God."

Maggie looked surprised. So I told her about Waynesville.

"If God wanted that," I said, "we should wonder about Him."

I could tell Maggie didn't want to go questioning God. Most folks with any sense didn't. Everything could unravel if you start doing that. And what good could come from it? I didn't want to doubt God either, but Jane had driven me there.

"Folks say if it weren't for her, the Government would've beaten us by now," Maggie said. "They say she's more important than Charles Winslow will ever be. You think that's true?"

"Yeah, I do. We owe her more . . ." I struggled to hold back tears.

Maggie was looking at me. Not with contempt or even concern. She watched me the way you watch game through the sights of your rifle. Waiting for the right moment.

"You in love with her?" she said.

I surprised myself by being able to look right at her as I said, "No. I thought so once. But that was just foolishness."

Just as easy, I could've said, "Yes. I still am. But that is just foolishness."

I had decided to tell a half-lie rather than a half-truth. The whole truth was I didn't know if I loved Jane, or even what love was. But I did know it was foolish to think about Jane that way.

Maggie was still. Watching. I guess she was making up her mind about me, and figuring what to do from here on. It was an effort to keep looking right at her, and that went on for a long time. Then she stood up and asked me if I would like some pie. I said I would.

A little while later, I thanked her for dinner, and we said our goodbyes. I wanted to touch her. Maybe she felt the same way, but there was still a wall between us. So I didn't. I just put on my hat and went out into the night, making sure I closed the door behind me.

Outside, it was getting colder, and a good wind had come up. The first snow couldn't be far away. I started walking, pulled down my hat, and turned up the collar of my coat. After a few steps, I stopped and turned. A light still shone in the window of Maggie's cabin. I still didn't believe that I would ever live in that cabin with Maggie, or raise children there. I didn't believe it would happen. But I would accept it as good fortune, a blessing, if it came. If I lived through the war. If the war ever ended. If.

Then I remembered talking with Jane's uncle. He told me not to be worrying on the future. "The only future you got is right now," he had said. And that was true. Gospel truth.

The light in the cabin went out. Maggie had gone to bed. I wished I were there with her. Not to be doing anything. No, I just wished to be warm, to drift into sleep unafraid and unalone. To dream good things.

But I was alone, in the dark, and getting colder. I turned and headed home. In two days, I would take my rifle and my bedroll and go back to the war. That was the only future I had.

22

And then the war was over. At least, that's what we thought.

The day before I was going to head back, my father and I had breakfast and went out to get some chores done. When we came back at midday, we found my mother in the kitchen, sitting in a chair, crying. Worried that something bad had happened, we rushed over to her and asked what was wrong. She started laughing and said the war was over.

She told us one of the Jameson boys came by on horseback with the news.

"How'd he know?" I said.

"His father heard it down at the trading store. War's over."

"Who did Mr. Jameson hear it from?" I said.

My mother didn't know. She hadn't asked. The Jameson boy had brought news she had been praying for. Folks are slow to question what they want to hear.

"This might not be true," I said, dropping into a chair.

My mother looked at me like I had slapped her. She needed to believe.

My father put a hand on her shoulder and said, "He's right. We have to find out."

She nodded. You could see her shoulder the burden again.

"I'm going to the Jameson place," I said. I was running out the door before they could say a word.

Mr. Jameson had heard the news from somebody else who had heard it from somebody else. He was so sure it was true that he had opened a bottle of whiskey to celebrate, even though the sun was still high in the sky. Full of good cheer, he offered me some. It was bad manners, but I said no thanks, and hurried home.

My parents and I sat at the kitchen table and talked. They wanted me to wait. Maybe more news would come along. But I needed to know.

Of course, I wanted to go right then, but that was foolishness. The sun was near down. Better to go in the morning.

"What about Maggie?" my mother said.

"You tell her for me," I said. Maggie and I had said what we had to say for now.

My mother looked disappointed, but she didn't argue.

I lay awake every minute of that night thinking in circles, waiting for the first sign of dawn.

My parents saw me off. My father gave me a firm handshake and my mother a hug. No tears. I went out the door and forced myself not to look back.

It all turned out to be unnecessary.

I had been walking for no more than a couple hours when I heard someone coming toward me. I got behind a tree and watched him come on. When he got a little closer, I recognized him. Stepping out where he could see me, my hands up and empty, I called his name, "Hey Weber!"

For a moment, he looked startled. Then he recognized me. "Hey!" he called and began laughing.

We shook hands and slapped one another on the back. I noticed he smelled of whiskey, but didn't appear drunk.

"Is it true?" I said.

"What?"

"The war. What else?"

"Hadn't you heard by now?"

"I heard. But didn't know for a fact. So it's really over?"

"Yeah. They told us Winslow made some kind of deal with the Government."

"Deal? What kind of deal?"

He shrugged. "Don't know, but the goddamn shooting stopped, and they said men with three years service was done and out."

"For good?"

"For as long as it lasts. All I know about is right now. And I'm going home!" We both grinned and slapped one another on the back again.

Then he frowned. "If you didn't know it was over, what you doing here?"

I explained how Campbell had sent me home a month ago. But I didn't explain why, and Weber didn't ask. He likely figured it was because I had gotten too nervous to be any damn good in a fight. It happened to a lot of us, but nobody talked about it.

"So you was headed back?" he said.

"Yeah. It was lucky running into you."

"Running into to me is always lucky."

We both laughed.

I wanted to head home right then, and invited Weber along, but he was real hungry and wondered if I had any food. I had some biscuits and bacon my mother had made. We made a little fire and started eating and talking.

He asked about Riley.

"Good," I said. "Last time I saw him anyways."

"What about that Jane Darcy? I heard you and Riley was with her for a while."

"Yeah." I shrugged, hoping he would take the hint.

"Is it true what everybody says about her?" Weber said. "Does God really tell her things?"

I shrugged again.

Weber still didn't take the hint and said, "I heard she--"

I cut him off. "What about the old squad? Harris? Stokes? Price?"

Weber didn't say anything for a long moment, and I could tell it was going to be bad. "All dead," he said.

I wanted to know more, but I said nothing. I left it up to him to say what he wanted.

"Just a few days after it all began. We got caught in some of that damn artillery. There was a big flash not ten yards from me. Price, Stokes, a couple others, just gone."

"Damn," I said in a whisper.

"Harris and me was together 'til a few weeks ago. An ambush went bad. He got all shot up."

I didn't say anything.

"Hung on for hours. Always was a stubborn sumbitch."

I was sorry I asked. It would've been better to talk about Jane than make Weber remember.

"Sorry," I said.

He shrugged. "Don't matter none."

Riley had said the same thing when I left. It mattered. Nothing could matter more.

We sat there for a long moment. Then I stood up, kicked out the fire, and said, "Come on. Let's go."

Weber stayed overnight, sleeping in my brother's old bed. In the morning, he wanted to be off for home. He didn't say how he felt, but I was a little sick and shaky from the whiskey the night before. My father had never been a drinking man, yet he counted my return with Weber as an occasion worthy of what he called "the snakebite medicine." We drank until midnight.

When we were full of the whiskey, Weber and I talked some about visiting or going hunting together sometime. But even as we were saying it, I knew it would never happen.

After some breakfast, I walked with Weber to where he would pick up a trail toward his home. We didn't say much. All our talking had been done the night before. We just shook hands, and he walked into the woods. I stood and watched him go. Just as he got to the top of a little rise, the sun came out from behind some clouds. He stopped, took off his hat, and tilted his head back to enjoy the feel of its warmth on his face. Then he turned toward me, gave me a wave with his hat, and went over the rise. The moment he disappeared, I had a strange feeling.

It was relief. Glad he was gone.

Now, you need to know I liked Weber. He was a good man and a good friend. If he asked my help, I would do whatever I could. But I knew him from the militia. He had seen me wake up from dreaming of the blue-eyed man. With Weber gone, I thought the militia and war belonged to the past, I could begin my life, my new life. I had a future again.

At least, that's what I thought.

23

Remembering those months at home always gives me a special feeling. I really don't know how to explain it, or even what to call it. When you put a name to something, it's like putting a nail through it. The nail holds it in place so you can find it again, but it takes the breathing life out of it too. The feeling I had was like seeing the first trickles of spring snowmelt coming through an ice-choked streambed. You see that trickle and know the world will soon be green and warm, full of life. Let's just say I was happy.

If you had been around, you wouldn't have seen much worth the seeing. I was 19 going on 20. I lived in the only home, and slept in the only bed, I had ever had. At dawn, I would be up and working, doing my chores, often until dark. If I could, I would visit Maggie and chop some wood. On a Friday or Saturday night, there might be a dance in one of the larger houses about. On Sunday, I would sit with my parents and Maggie in church. And when I wasn't too tired in the evenings, I would sit close to the fire and read a book. And maybe you wouldn't have noticed, but I had stopped carrying my rifle everywhere.

The most important thing for me in those days was Maggie. I don't remember when or how it happened, but Maggie and I, and everyone around us too, stopped wondering if we would be married. Instead, we knew. That knowing was the warmth in the heart of that winter. It was the newness of my new life.

Now and then, I would have a restless night filled with thoughts of the past, with the tangle of things I had done and failed to do. I would sit in the dark, thinking of Jane and Riley, and all the rest of it. I couldn't make the thoughts go away. But I could stand it because I knew if I held on, dawn would set me free. And that was how it was until a cold gray day in March.

I was chopping wood when Riley came around a corner of the house. For a moment, I wondered if he was real. Then I leaned the ax against the house and went over to him. I was so surprised I didn't know what to say or do.

"Hey," he said and stuck out his hand.

I shook it and said, "Hey."

Then happiness pushed everything else aside. My friend was alive. He had come through. I threw my arms around him and pounded him on the back. He did the same, but with only one hand. The other still held a rifle.

It wasn't till I had him inside, getting warm at the fire, that I remembered where Riley lived. He couldn't be on his way home. It was in the opposite direction. He could've only come here to find me, to tell me something. And the thought of what it might be frightened me.

I sat down facing him. He was looking into the fire. For one long strange moment, I was sure he had come to tell me Jane was dead. In that moment, I was back on that dark street, the soldiers shooting at us, Jane going down, and I was waiting to see if the world would keep on turning.

Then I was just as sure Jane was alive and that she had sent Riley to get me. No, not this time, I thought. I'm not coming this time.

"Tell me," I said.

"Jane wants you to come back."

"Come back? What for? The war's over. The soldiers are gone."

"No. Not over. Not gone. It just stopped for a spell. Jane says the war will start again in the spring."

"So that's what Jane says. What about Campbell? What about Winslow? What do they say?"

"Don't know what they say. But Jane says--"

"Jane says?! I've had enough of what Jane says. I don't give a damn what she says anymore!" By the time I was finished, I was standing up, shouting at him.

Riley didn't get angry. He just sat there and took it.

"I'm sorry," I said, sitting down again. "I didn't mean to . . ." I trailed off, feeling foolish.

"I know. I told her you'd feel this way. Told her it was a waste of time. But she wanted me to ask. So I asked." Then he looked into the fire.

"I'm getting married in the spring," I said, trying to get us talking about something else.

"Good. What was her name? Maggie?"

"Yeah."

We were quiet for a while. He looked into the fire, scratching his beard.

I told him about seeing Weber, and about Stokes and Harris. Riley said he knew and told me Carl was dead.

"Soldiers?"

114

"No, his heart just gave out. He was too old to go running around the mountains. I don't know how he lasted as long as he did. He was more than sixty."

I nodded. I knew they had likely buried him in some forgotten hole. I wondered if, at the very end, he still thought helping Jane was the best thing he had ever done. Too late to ask.

We were quiet again for a while.

"If they call up the militia again," I said, "I'll go but . . ."

"I know," Riley said. "I'd do the same in your shoes." Then he stood up and walked over to his hat, bedroll, and rifle.

I realized he was getting ready to leave.

"Come on," I said. "Stay a while. Have dinner with us and sleep in a real bed. My father will want to break out the whiskey."

Riley smiled at this, thanked me, and said he had to go, started toward the door.

"Don't go," I said, feeling bad about the way I had shouted at him. But I realized that had nothing to do with it. The bad feeling was from the choice I had made.

"Wish I could," he said, already at the door putting out his hand. We shook hands without saying anything more, and he went out. I stepped outside and watched him walk away and go around the corner of the house. He didn't look back.

After a while, I guess I went back to chopping wood. I don't remember. Work had always made my tangled thoughts go away. Not this time. I was walking about, doing chores, and eating the evening meal with my parents, but all the while listening to gunfire and shouts, seeing blood, smelling smoke.

That night, I didn't want to go to sleep. I knew who would be waiting for me there. Ever since I had started for home, he had been close. He was stalking me, staying just beyond the edge of my thoughts. So I sat in the dark and looked at my bed, wondering how long I could stay awake. But I realized that was foolish. The dead have no need of rest. The blue-eyed man had all the time in the world. He could wait.

So I lay down and closed my eyes, trembling with the fear. But finally sleep came. Then the dream.

I was alone, walking through piney woods at twilight. The trees were immense, thick, tall, and very old. There was no undergrowth, just a thick layer of needles covering easy rolling ground. It was a beautiful soft summer evening.

Twilight faded to darkness. But I kept walking. It was too dark to see which direction I should go. But I realized--as if I knew this was a dream-- any direction would take me where I had to go.

At first, I could hear all the sounds of the woods at night, crickets, and birds, now and then the soft scurry of something four-legged getting out of my path. But all the sounds went away when I caught sight of the fire. Someone had made a camp and built a fire. That's where I was going.

As I moved toward it, the silence of the woods, of the whole world, deepened and swallowed me. I couldn't hear my boots on the pine needles. I couldn't even hear my own breathing.

The fire was in the center of a clearing. As soon as I stepped out from the trees, I felt afraid. I moved forward in a crouch. But no one was there. No camp, no bedrolls, no cooking pots. Just a big fire, set in the middle of a perfect circle of stones, burning in absolute silence. It gave no heat, only light. Cold silent light.

I squatted by the fire until I saw movement on the other side. It was a man carrying a rifle in the crook of his left arm. As he moved into the light, I realized it wasn't a man. It was Jane--Jane just as I had first seen her. The same baggy britches. The same chopped up hair. The fire reflected in her eyes.

I stood up, and we looked at each other across the fire. Then I felt she was asking me for something, asking with her eyes. And I answered without words. I couldn't, or just wouldn't, give what she was asking for. She appeared to understand this, but it made her sad. She nodded and turned to go back into the darkness. Before she disappeared, she stopped and looked at me again. Then she was gone.

I started to turn away, but I saw someone else coming out of the dark. Expecting it to be Jane's uncle, I smiled. But it wasn't her uncle. He looked at me, his blue eyes steady and calm. For a long time, we didn't move. Then he stepped into the fire and nodded. An invitation. I nodded and stepped into the fire as well.

It was cold in there, colder than any winter night I had ever known. The cold didn't surprise me or even bother me. But the silence was replaced by a storm of sound, a maddening roar that swept away everything, but hatred and rage.

The blue-eyed man and I stood still for a moment, gathering our strength. And we leapt at one another.

Then I was sitting up in my bed. My blankets were on the floor and I shaking with cold. After the light and roar of the fire, I was shocked by the darkness and silence of my room. I grabbed a blanket and wrapped it around my shoulders.

My hands were shaking as I put on my boots, loaded my rifle, and gathered other things I would need. My hands were still shaking when I wrote the note to my parents and to Maggie. Leaving a note, of course, wasn't right. But I knew they would ask me why I was going. I had no answer. And they would talk me into staying. It would be easy because I wanted to stay and was afraid to go. I had to leave. The note just said that I was sorry and that I hoped to be back soon. I left it on the kitchen table and went out the back door into the cold an hour before first light.

I didn't stop shaking until the sun was well up, warming me as I climbed the trail, a steep trail that would take me back to where I would find Riley. And Jane.

24

It took me almost two days to catch up with Riley. I found him just before dark. He had heard someone coming and waited behind a tree. When he saw it was me, he stepped out and smiled. We shook hands.

He never asked why, and I didn't say. I guess he thought it enough that I had come. Talk didn't matter. But as we bedded down that night, I asked him a question.

"Riley, what's if she's wrong?"

"Jane?"

"Yeah."

"Wrong about what?"

"The war. The Government. God. Everything."

He didn't say anything for a long time, but I could feel he was still awake, thinking about it.

"Don't matter none," he said. "I made a promise."

Maybe I should've told him it wasn't that simple for me, but there was no use talking about it. So I shut up and let Riley drift off to sleep. After a while, I could hear that familiar soft snore of his. But I lay awake for a long time and watched the stars wheel past the treetops.

Jane was sitting next to a fire at Central Camp, eating some stew, when we found her. She looked up, saw us, and smiled.

I was expecting we would talk about why I had left and why I had come back. God knows I had thought about it enough, making up little speeches on the long walk from home. But when we actually looked at each other, I knew, knew for a fact, we would never talk about any of that.

Jane just pointed to the stew pot. "Help yourself."

Riley, who was already at the pot, filling a plate with stew, looked up at me and winked.

I didn't know what to say. But I was hungry. So I got some stew and sat down to eat.

And that was that.

The next morning I went to talk to Campbell.

He didn't look well. Sitting in a small shed, he had a blanket draped over his shoulders. There were dark circles under his eyes.

"What the hell are you doing here?" he said.

I told him Jane had asked me to come back.

"Why?" he said.

"She thinks the war's not over."

"I know. Don't you think she's told me that?" He sounded angry.

"Yes, Sir. She's likely told you a dozen times."

He snorted. "A dozen? More like a hundred." He sat back in his chair and readjusted his blanket. "Sorry to be sharp with you. Not your fault."

"Yes, Sir."

"I know why she wants you back. What I want to know is why the hell you came."

I didn't have an answer to that. Anything I said about the dream and the blue-eyed man would just sound like foolishness to Campbell.

"Well . . ." I said, stalling, trying to think.

He leaned forward in his chair.

Then I remembered what Riley had told me.

"I made a promise," I said. It was as true as anything I could think to say.

"All right," he said, leaning back and resettling the blanket, "you made a promise. But I hope you know some promises are damn hard to keep. And some are best not kept."

I knew. Or thought I did.

The next day, Jackson and a few men came into camp on horseback. I hadn't seen Jackson since the beginning of the war when he had been so angry about Jane. Now, he looked pretty damn pleased with himself. At least he did until he caught sight of Jane. Then there was a flash of trouble in his eyes. After a moment, he turned away and went back to being pleased with himself, or at least trying to look that way.

I glanced at Jane. She was watching Jackson with hard eyes.

Later that day, Jane got word to come and see Campbell. She told me to come along.

"You sure?" I said.

"Let's go."

We went into Campbell's shed. Seated on the other side of a table were Campbell, who did not look happy, and Jackson, who did. Jackson was sitting in a bigger chair at the center. Campbell was sitting to one side. He didn't have the blanket over his shoulders, but he still looked tired and sick.

Jane said hello and took a chair at the table. Jackson gave me an annoyed look. I guess he was still wondering why I was there. I stood at the wall, behind Jane.

Jane spoke first. "Where's Winslow?"

Campbell looked down at some papers on the table and let Jackson answer. "General Winslow is busy with other matters. He asked me . . . and Colonel Campbell, of course, to discuss a few . . . a few matters with you."

"I don't understand," she said.

Jackson smiled. "As you know, the Government has offered a peace treaty on very good terms, and General Winslow, with the advice of the Council of Elders, has accepted. I am here, on his behalf, to ask your support."

"Peace treaty? Victory is the only peace."

"Well . . . I can understand why you might feel that way, but General Winslow has to consider what is best for our people in the long-run. And that's very complicated."

"What terms?"

"The Government is offering us many things that can make the lives of our people better. Think about our people being able to sell the things we grow and make. Think about the things the Government has. Medicine and doctors, trucks, electricity, and even radio. Think about what having even some of these things could mean for us."

Jane said nothing.

"Let me show you something." Jackson put a black box on the table and worked a crank that stuck out of one side. Then he turned a knob on the front. There was a click and then music came out of the box. It was a radio, just like the ones from before the Plague. Jackson let the radio play for a minute and then turned the knob again. A click and then silence.

I was amazed, and I felt the pull of my old daydreams of the life people had before the Plague. Jane's voice jerked me back.

"What do they want from us?" she said.

"The Government wants the big road, I-40."

She looked at Campbell. "But what about what Carl did? They can't use the road anymore, can they?"

Campbell looked over at Jackson. It was clear enough then that Jackson was running things now.

"Yes," Campbell said, "right now the road is useless. It will take time, but they can definitely rebuild it."

"So they can attack us again."

Jackson held up his hands as if to calm Jane down. "We keep control of the high ground surrounding the road and, of course, they guarantee our security and independence."

"Guarantee?"

"Yes," Jackson said. "The Government promises not to attack us. And, of course, we promise not to attack them."

"You believe their promises? After everything they've done? After all the blood? You must be fools."

Jackson looked angry and then seemed to get hold of himself. "No. We're not fools. So here it is, plain and simple. We can't beat them. We've slowed them down, for now. But if we keep fighting, they will just bring more men and better weapons until they destroy us. They'll slaughter every man, woman, and child in these mountains, and take the road. But if we make a deal, right now, at least we can get something. We have to do the best we can for our people. We can't win."

"You're too ready to quit."

"You're too ready to gamble the lives of our people," Jackson said. "If we fight and lose, we lose everything. Everything."

Jane did not say anything for a while. Jackson and Campbell just sat waiting for her to speak.

"I don't know much about the time before, but I do know this," she said. "The Indians once had all this land. Then the Whites came and wanted the land. They gave the Indians gifts. They made promises—"

"What's your point?" Jackson said.

"But the Whites forgot the promises and took what they wanted. The Indians were fools to believe the Whites, and you are fools to believe the Government. They want our land. They'll take it. And you're letting them."

Campbell looked down at his papers, silent. Jackson stared at Jane.

"I want to talk to Winslow," Jane said, standing up. "When can I see him?"

"I speak for General Winslow," Jackson said. "And the decision has been made. He wants your support."

"No." She turned and walked out of the shed. I stood and gave Campbell a hard look. He didn't seem to notice. Then I followed her.

She was waiting for me. I walked up to her. Before I could say anything, she grabbed my collar and pulled my ear close to her mouth.

"Now we fight," she said.

A few days later, Jane, Riley, and I were sitting, staring into our fire when Campbell walked out of the darkness.

"May I join you?" he said.

It was the first time I had seen him since that meeting, and I wasn't going to miss my chance to tell him off. I rose to my feet. "You know she's right. Why don't you help her?"

Both Campbell and Jane ignored me.

"Have a seat, Colonel," she said.

He nodded and sat on the ground. I sat down too, feeling foolish as well as angry.

"I know what you're planning," he said.

"You do?" she said.

"Yes. You're going to keep on fighting. You're going to get as many men as you can and attack the soldiers. Wreck the treaty and start the war again."

Jane said nothing.

He knew. This was our plan. This was what Riley and I had told some other men in camp whom we trusted. We asked them to think about coming with us, to spread the word. Somebody had told Campbell.

"Do not do this," he said. "Do not. Please."

"You know this deal with the Government is a mistake. It's a bargain with the Devil."

"Yes," he said. "It's a mistake. But back when all this began you asked me if I would defy Winslow to attack the Government."

"I remember."

"Do you remember what I said?"

"Yes. You said wouldn't divide our people."

"And only then did you agreed to work with me."

Jane was silent.

"So what's different now?" Campbell said. "Why are you willing to divide us?"

Riley and I exchanged a look. I had forgotten about that. I could tell he had too.

"I can only ask you, all of you, to trust me," she said. "This is what I must do." Then she looked at me, asking for my help.

For a moment, I felt myself waver, letting my doubts rise. But I nodded.

She looked at Riley. He looked away, squinting, scratching his beard. "You can count on me."

He looked sad. Maybe he could see, better than I, where this would lead us.

"I'm sorry," Campbell said. "The treaty is a mistake. The Government's just playing for time. They'll come after us again. And I've told Winslow and Jackson this. Many, many times."

"So why don't you help us?" I said.

He turned to me, "Because my duty, my duty, is to carry out the decisions our leaders make. Whether I like it or not."

"Even when they are dead wrong?" I said.

"Yes, because we have to stick together. David Winslow made us a people. We were united. When we really needed it, we were strong."

He turned back to Jane. "Do this and you'll be giving the Government just what it wants. They want us divided. They want us weak."

Jane stood up and reached for her rifle, David Winslow's rifle. For a long moment, she looked at it, holding it in both hands.

She walked around the fire to Campbell and handed him the rifle. "Please, give this back to Winslow. Thank him for the loan of it."

Then she stepped back. "You can tell him I'm going home. You can tell him I'm going to fight. Tell him whatever your duty requires. But I'll do what God requires of me."

Campbell looked at the rifle in his hands. Then he stood and walked away, leaving the three of us at the fire, surrounded by darkness.

25

I grabbed Jane by the arm and shouted in her ear, "Pull back!"

Just then, a burst of .50 caliber started tearing up a nearby tree, showering us with dust and splinters. Terrified, I closed my eyes and pressed myself as flat as I could against the ground.

When I opened my eyes again, Jane's face was just inches away. She was screaming, "No! No! Attack!"

There was an odd look in her eyes. I had seen it before in men fighting hand-to-hand, men straining to choke or drive a knife in deep. She wanted to hurl herself, to hurl all of us, at the soldiers. She wanted to destroy the soldiers, consequences be damned. I could not let her do that to herself, or to us.

We had to get out of there before the soldiers sent men up to finish us. I shouted, "Pull back! Pull back!"

No one hesitated. They all began crawling away. I grabbed Jane by the arm and started pulling her in the direction we had to go. She shook her head, whipping it back and forth, and wrenched her arm away from me. For the briefest instant, I wondered if she might shoot me. But she didn't, and I grabbed her by the arm again. This time, she came with me.

As soon as we could, we got up and started running. We were sloppy about looking for soldiers following us, about covering our retreat. We just ran.

When we got back to the rally point, I was amazed that we hadn't lost anyone. We were all shaky, sweating, and gasping for breath. Two men had dry heaves--nothing coming up because we hadn't eaten much lately. Slumped against a tree, my heart pounding, I knew that another man, perhaps two, would slip away in the night. Gone home.

Things had started well enough. We had fewer men than we hoped, but still enough for three squads. It was enough to begin. Jane believed that word of what we were doing would spread that others would join us, or start fighting the Government on their own.

At first, we surprised the soldiers working on the road. They had been told the fighting was over. So it was easy to hit them and get away. Then, of course, the soldiers got careful, posting more guards and using heavier weapons, like the big machine guns. Still, we held the initiative. We attacked when and where we chose. We had the advantage.

But soon, lots of folks stopped helping us. They started turning us away when we asked for food or shelter. People were tired of war, sick of fear and death. They wanted some peace.

Then the Government did something very clever. They sent doctors with loads of medicines into our mountains. And it was all free. The few soldiers who came with the doctors didn't point their rifles at anyone. Our people would walk for days and wait for hours to get medicine for their children and grandchildren, and for their old folks. The Government also sent trucks full of food, clothing, and shoes. They gave it all away, free. And they gave out radios, like the one Jackson had showed Jane. The Government wanted our people to hear news of the world beyond our mountains, the news the Government wanted them to hear.

While the Government was giving all these things to our people, it sent special soldiers to hunt us down. These were not like most of the conscripts, who had been forced to fight. These were the soldiers who were good at war, who had a taste for it.

Like I said, we started with three squads, but soon, one disappeared. When we found it, every man was dead. The bloated bodies were lined up in a neat row. A message.

After this, men began to leave. In the morning, they were just gone. We lost so many that we had to combine our two remaining squads. Then more left.

I wondered how it had gotten this bad. But I knew. I had always known.

Our men had followed Jane because she was so sure of herself, so sure she would make just the right choice at just the right time, so sure she would triumph against impossible odds. She did that so often that they came to believe far more than luck was at work. They believed God was with her.

But then she began to make bad choices. Failure made her courage and certainty seem foolish. The men who had slipped away in the night had decided God was not with Jane. They reckoned she had just run out of luck.

That's what had happened this time. If we had not pulled out when we did, we might all be dead. No one said it, but we all knew Jane had almost killed us. If not today, then tomorrow. It was just a matter of time.

We moved deep into the woods to hide for the night. We could not have a fire. It would give away our position. We sat in the darkness, slapping at insects, while we ate what little food we had left. In the silence, I sensed a cold anger among the men. God knows, I felt that way.

I thought how nice it would be to eat a meal, a real meal, with my family again. To sit in church next to Maggie. To dance with her. If I hadn't left home to follow Jane, Maggie and I would be married by now. We would be in bed together. I had ruined all that, of course. If I ever made it home, Maggie wouldn't be, shouldn't be, waiting for someone like me.

The sound of Jane's voice brought me back.

"I know," she said. "I know you're tired. You've every reason to leave. But I'm asking you to believe, just a little longer. God is at work in this, all of this. Please have faith."

There was a long silence. I couldn't see the faces of our men in the dark. I could feel them fighting to have the faith Jane asked for, fighting the pull of something in their past or their future.

I wanted to tell Jane she had asked too much for too long. She had gotten too many of us killed, killed for nothing. She had no right to ask us to follow her again. The price was too high.

I wanted to say all these angry things. Instead, what came out of my mouth was, "I will."

A moment later, I heard Riley's voice in the dark. "I will too." Then one by one, all of us agreed with a "Me too," or a "Yeah," or a "Reckon so."

When they were done, Jane just said, "Thank you. God bless you." I felt her hand touch my arm for just a moment. She had gotten what she wanted from us. We would go on fighting, and I had made it possible.

When I woke at first light, all the men were still there, one on watch, the rest still sleeping. Jane was up, kneeling in the woods, as she always did, whispering her insistent prayers. I wondered if she had been as close to the brink as the rest of us, as I had been, the night before.

I would never know.

26

When it happened, I was half asleep, plodding along with my head down, dumbly watching the boot heels of the man walking about ten feet in front of me. I was tired and thinking about food. The man in front of me stopped. I stopped too and looked up to see why. Just then, his head exploded. A sudden spray of blood and meat.

I remember feeling rather than hearing the roar of automatic rifles, and bullets ripping up the air around me. As I lifted my rifle, there was a huge white flash a few yards in front of me.

The next thing I remember is being face down in the dirt. I raised my head just a little and saw several soldiers walking slowly out of the trees, stepping over the torn-up bodies of my friends. I could see the soldiers were talking to one another, but couldn't hear them. I couldn't hear anything. None of them seemed to take any notice of me.

There was movement to my left, and I looked that way. Two soldiers had Jane. One was pulling the rifle out of her hands, and the other had an arm around her throat, a chokehold.

I tried to get up, but the ground seemed to tilt and slide away, and I went down hard on my hands and knees. The soldier had gotten the rifle away from her, and she was struggling, using both hands to pull the arm from around her throat. That's when she caught sight of me, pulled hard on the arm, and managed to shout something while shaking her head.

I was almost on my feet again when a soldier stepped out from behind a tree. He brought a rifle butt toward my head. I could see it coming, so fast yet slow enough for me to remember the scratches on the stock. I just watched it come closer and wondered why I wasn't trying to duck.

When I opened my eyes again, it was night, and the world was tilting first to the left, then to the right, and to left again. I was slumped against a tree with my hands bound behind me, and my ankles tied together with a leather strap. My arms and legs hurt. Everything hurt. I could see the light of a fire off to my left, but when I turned my head to look, I felt a brilliant flash inside my head. I closed my eyes and tried to slip away from the pain and hide in the darkness.

It was morning when I came back. I was still slumped against the tree with my hands and ankles bound. Everything still hurt, especially my wrists and hands, but I didn't feel sick or dizzy anymore. I was tired, hungry, and thirsty. In front of me was a small patch of muddy ground about ten feet across with trees on the other side. I didn't see anyone.

Then the memories: The ambush. Jane. The rifle butt. For a moment, I had to fight a helpless panic. That's when a soldier walked into view and squatted in front of me. He didn't say anything, but looked at me close, studying me. I just stared at him, feeling unsure and slow in the head. Without looking away, he called to someone I couldn't see, "He's awake."

A voice off to my left said, "Good. Give him some water." The voice was familiar, but I couldn't place it.

The squatting soldier stepped away and came back with a canteen. He screwed off the top and tipped some water into my mouth. I swallowed, and he gave me some more. As I swallowed that, he poured some over my face. The water helped me feel more like myself. More awake anyway. Then that soldier stepped back, and another squatted down in front of me. It took a moment to recognize him.

"Remember me, boy?" he said.

"Lieutenant Hobbes. Jane let you go."

"Right. That got me a promotion. I'm a Captain now." He smiled.

"Is she alive?" I said,

"Yeah. The others are dead. You'd be too, but I wanted to talk a little."

"Before you shoot me?" I said. I knew, knew for a fact, Hobbes was going to kill me. The strange thing was it didn't bother me, not near as much as other times I thought I might die. Maybe it was losing Jane and Riley, maybe it was being angry, or maybe it was getting busted in the head, but somehow I didn't care.

He shrugged. "Yeah. I'm going to shoot you. That's what you were going to do to me, wasn't it?"

"We were. Too bad."

He smiled. "I ought to tell you there is a way to stay alive. Just swear allegiance to the United States--"

"Fuck you."

"Of course, you'd spend the next few years at hard labor, maybe working in a mine. We call it rehabilitation. But most die before their time is up."

"Glad I made the right choice. What'd you want to talk about?"

"You in a hurry to get shot?"

"Can't say as I'm enjoying your company much."

He laughed. "Okay. Why did she do it?"

"She told you."

"You mean God? God told her to fight us?"

"Yeah, God."

He shook his head. "You believe God talked to her?"

"I don't know. I really don't. But she believes."

"If you don't know, why'd you follow her around like some trained dog?"

"None of your fucking business," I said. "But I'll tell you this. Fighting you sumbitches was the best thing I ever did."

"But your leaders made peace with us. And Jane didn't. Your friends are dead because of her."

"No. My friends are dead because of you. She kept fighting because you slaughtered women and children. She kept fighting because you won't leave us alone. She kept fighting because your 'peace' is just another way of making war."

"There's only room for one government on this continent. We'll do whatever is necessary."

"No matter how many folks you have to kill."

He shrugged. "Whatever is necessary."

We looked at each other for a long moment. I don't know what he saw, or didn't see, in my eyes, but I couldn't find the least glimmer of a troubled conscience in his. I wondered if he lost it back in the dark hungry days after the Plague, or if the Government took it from him later. Or maybe he never had a conscience. Anyway, it didn't matter.

I said, "What's going to happen to Jane?"

"She'll be tried for her crimes."

"Crimes? What crimes?"

"Treason. Murder. Terrorism. War crimes. You know, she killed a lot of innocent people in that Waynesville fire. Anyway, I'm sure they'll think of something good."

"Why don't you just shoot her and be done with it?"

"No, a public trial of someone like Jane reminds people of an important truth."

"Truth? What truth?"

"You can't fight the future."

"If you're the future, I don't want to live in it."

"Don't worry," he said, smiling. "You won't."

Hobbes stood up and called the soldier who had given me the water. This man took the strap from my ankles and then grabbed me by one arm and hauled me to my feet. I thought my shoulder would pop out of the socket, and I shouted, "Shit!" Then he pushed me forward, and I fell hard, landing on my side in the mud. The man gave me a kick in the gut to knock the wind out of me. Then he hauled me up again and dragged me along, stumbling and gasping, until we got to the edge of a gully. At the bottom, a stream rushed past over rocks.

"This is good," Hobbes called out loud enough to be heard over the stream. The man threw me down on the ground and stepped away. I looked up and saw Hobbes holding a pistol.

Now like I said, I knew this would happen. I knew Hobbes he would shoot me, and I accepted it. But it was still a strange thing to watch the last moment of your life unfold. What I saw was a man, dressed in black, standing in a beam of morning sunlight under a bright canopy of trees. He had a smile on his face as he raised the pistol. I couldn't hear anything, save my gasps for air and the hissing roar of the stream behind me. It may sound strange, but I didn't bother to pray. I reckoned God had long since made up His mind about me.

The shot hit Hobbes in the neck. A jet of blood flew out in front of him, and he stumbled forward. The pistol fell from his hand as his knees buckled. Hobbes pitched forward and hit the ground with his face.

The soldier and I were so surprised that we didn't move. But after a moment, he went for the pistol Hobbes had dropped. My hands were still bound, and I was on my side. All I could do was kick his knee as he went past. He cried out and stumbled. He still got the pistol, but I had slowed him down enough for the next shot to find his chest. Just left of center. The heart. Pistol in hand, the soldier stumbled backward until he went over the edge into the gully.

I lay on my side, breathing hard. I saw some brush pushed aside. It was Riley. He went to Hobbes and kicked him, checking for signs of life. I rolled on my belly so Riley could free my hands. Then he helped me up. My legs shook, and I almost fell down.

"Can you travel?" Riley said.

"Can't stay here."

To make it harder for the soldiers to track us, we went down into the gully and moved upstream for a while before cutting into the woods. We kept going until dark and never saw any sign the soldiers were after us. Then we hid in an old tumbledown house.

Sitting in the dark, he told me that he was on rear guard, walking well behind us when the ambush hit. By the time he got close, it was over. He figured we were all dead until he saw a couple soldiers dragging me away. So he hid nearby and waited for a chance.

"Nice shooting," I said. "You got the first one right through the neck. You remember him?"

"Hobbes. Should've killed that bastard back when."

"Better late than never."

Riley was quiet, but I knew his next question.

"They took Jane alive," I said. "I saw it. Hobbes told me they were going to put her on trial."

"Where'd they take her?"

"Don't know. Hobbes didn't say. Maybe he didn't know."

"You get some rest," Riley said. "I'll keep watch. We'll figure out what to do in the morning."

"Yeah. Thanks."

I used Riley's bedroll and lay down. I knew I needed to sleep, but I couldn't let myself go. I just lay there and remembered it all, again and again. I remembered one thing I hadn't told Riley.

It was when Jane caught sight of me, struggling to my feet, trying to get to her. She had managed to shout something while shaking her head. But I couldn't hear. I went over that moment again and again in my memory. I watched her lips move and tried to understand what she was trying to tell me.

Then I realized what it was. She had shouted, "No!"

She hadn't wanted me to help her.

I wouldn't tell Riley this.

I wouldn't tell anyone.

I would get her back.

27

"No!" Campbell shouted, slamming his hand down on the table. "Now get the hell out of this camp!"

Riley and I stood on the other side of the table. Through the window, I could see men outside stopping to look, wondering about the shouting.

"All right, Colonel," I said. "We'll get! But God damn you, and God damn Charles fucking Winslow, for not helping Jane."

"Amen!" Riley said.

"I ought to have you two shot for desertion," shouted Campbell. He leaned across the table, glaring at us.

We glared back.

Then he winked.

Confused, I looked at Riley. Just as confused, Riley looked back at me.

Campbell shouted, "Lieutenant Penland! Get these two out of here. Now!" Campbell turned away, done with us.

Soon we were out of the camp and in the woods, heading down the same path we had so often climbed with Jane.

"What do we do now?" I said to Riley.

"Don't know," he said.

We kept walking until it started getting dark. Then we stopped to build a fire.

It had taken a week for us to get to Campbell. In that time, Jane could've been taken anywhere in government territory. Riley and I had no way of knowing. We thought Campbell might know where she was, or how to get the Government to let her go. We thought he would want to help Jane. Instead, he turned us down flat.

Then he winked at us.

"What was that wink about?" Riley said.

"Don't know."

We fell silent. Riley may have been thinking about what we should do, but I was remembering: A soldier pulling the rifle from Jane's hands, another dragging her away. Then the rifle butt coming toward my head--

A sound of movement out in the dark. Riley grabbed his rifle, and I picked up a big stick as a club.

A voice called out, "Don't shoot. Campbell sent me."

Campbell? I thought.

"Come on then. Slow," Riley said.

A man came out of the darkness into the fire light. His hands were up. He had a canvas bag in one hand and a bedroll in the other.

When he got closer, I recognized him. It was Lieutenant Penland, who had taken us out of camp.

"Campbell sent you?" I said.

"Yeah," Penland said. "He wants to help."

"Then why the fuck didn't he say so?" I said.

"Politics," Penland said. "Jane tried to wreck the treaty with the Government. Besides, Winslow's afraid she wanted his job. So he won't do a thing for her."

"That sumbitch," Riley said. "She saved his ass."

Penland nodded. "Campbell agrees. But if he does anything to help Jane, Winslow will make Jackson his Chief of Staff, and Jane will get no help at all."

"So that explains the wink," I said.

"Wink?" Penland said.

"Never mind," Riley said. "How's Campbell gonna help?"

"Jane's in Asheville," Penland said. He pulled out an old map from inside his coat and showed us. South of the city, there was a big green area surrounding something marked 'Biltmore House.' Penland said, "Way before the Plague a rich man built a big house there, a kind of palace. The Government took it over."

"How do you know Jane's there?" I said.

"That's what the Government is saying on the radio," he said

"What else do they say?" I said.

"They're going to try her for murder, terrorism, and other things. Sometimes, they talk about how crazy she is because she talks to God. And they say she refuses to confess. 'Remains defiant,' is what they say."

"'Remains defiant,'" Riley said. "That's Jane."

"If we know where she is," I said, "how do we get her out?"

"We don't know," Penland said. "But there's a group fighting the Government. It's called the Underground. We've had contact with them for a while, and they might want to help."

"What'll they do?" Riley said.

"They might give you a place to hide, food, information. But more than that . . ." Penland shrugged.

"How do we find them?" I said.

Penland told us to go to a particular house after dark. He showed it to us on the map. One of us should go to the door, say his name was Watson, and that he was looking for Holmes.

"Watson looking for Holmes," I said. "A code?"

"Yeah. If they say nobody named Holmes is there, it's not safe. Get away."

"What do we do then?" Riley said.

"You're on your own. That's our only way to get in contact with them."

Riley let out a low whistle. We were climbing pretty far up a shaky tree.

Penland gave us the map and the canvas bag, which held two pistols, extra ammunition, and some food. He handed me the bedroll and said, "Campbell noticed you didn't have one of these."

"Thank him for me," I said.

"One last thing," Penland said. "I'm sorry, but if you get caught, Campbell will deny you got help from us."

"The Colonel shouldn't worry," Riley said. "They'll likely shoot us without much fuss."

"Please thank him for everything," I said.

Penland nodded. "I'll pray for you." He shook hands with us and walked away, back toward the camp.

Riley and I spent some time checking the pistols and looking at the map. Then we sat, gazing into the fire.

"How in the world are we gonna do this?" I said.

"What was it Jane used to say? 'If it's God's will, He'll make a way. I just have to be ready.'"

"Are you ready?"

He smiled. "Ready? I was born ready." It was an old joke.

"No, for real. Their headquarters. The belly of the beast."

His smile went away. "Can't see any way around it."

We were quiet for a bit.

"You know," I said, "I feel bad cause I got you into this."

"Got me into this?"

"Yeah, back at the beginning. The Captain told me I'd need another man. I picked you."

He laughed. "Sure, you got me into this. But I got you back into it. Even went to get you. Remember?"

I shrugged. He had a point.

"So I reckon we're even," he said.

"Yeah. Reckon so."

We sat and watched until the fire burned down to embers.

28

"So that's Asheville," I said.

"Yeah," Riley said. "Ever been down here?"

"No. You?"

"No. A cousin came down once to do some trading. The sumbitch got drunk and lost everything in a card game."

"And you wonder why city folk think Hillbillies are dumb."

Daylight was fading behind the mountains to our west, and the lights were coming on in the city. From the hillside where we stood, I looked toward the southern edge of the city, where the Government headquarters was, where Jane might be. We were too far away, and it was too dark to see anything.

Riley and I had said little in the days we had been traveling. Until we contacted the Underground, we did not know a damn thing. So why talk? Tomorrow we would find the house and we would know something. Good or bad, we would know.

We settled in for the night without building a fire. We were too close to the Government's army for that. Riley took the first watch, as he always did, and I went to sleep. I dreamt of the soldiers taking Jane away. She was in pain. I could see it in her eyes. Then I saw the rifle in her hands the moment before they took it away from her. And then, it wasn't in her hands, but in mine, and I was giving it to her. Then, it wasn't a rifle. It was a flower. We were in a meadow, and I was handing her a flower I had picked just for her.

She didn't look the way I had known her. Her hair was long, and she wore a dress. She smiled at me as I handed her the flower. I going to say something, something I was frightened to say. And then, she asked me if I wanted more eggs. We were in a kitchen, a kitchen like my mother's,

135

and Jane was putting fried eggs on my plate. I looked around the table, and there were two children. Our children.

I turned to smile at Jane, but we weren't in the kitchen anymore. We were in the woods. Jane was ahead, wearing her old clothes again, running from me. I called to her, and she turned. Then she was holding up one hand as if I should stop, as if I should go back. She shook her head and shouted something.

Then soldiers were everywhere, all shooting at me. I could hear the bullets go by and feel the way they made the air move.

Then the rifle butt was coming toward me, and again I watched, and again I wondered why I didn't duck. It hit me. Then I saw myself kneeling on the ground, my head bent forward. I couldn't see my face. The soldiers were standing around me, and one had a pistol to my head. I recognized him. It was Hobbes. He had a pistol to my head and was going to shoot me. I wondered where Jane was.

But then the kneeling man wasn't me anymore. It was Riley. Hobbes fired the pistol, and Riley's head exploded. I could hear Jane screaming. I looked at Hobbes, but the man with the smoking pistol was now me.

I was awake, sitting up and breathing hard. Riley was looking at me. I held up a hand and said, "A dream."

Riley nodded and turned away to let me settle down.

But I wasn't going to sleep, not that night. So I got up and relieved Riley.

He fell asleep, and I was alone in the dark. I thought about the dream even though I knew I shouldn't. I had the urge to wake Riley up and tell him about it. I had the urge, but I didn't. It's just a dream, I thought. Just a dream.

The next day we found the house. It was on the edge of town, and only one building nearby seemed occupied. Riley and I hid in a thicket with a view of the front door. We waited until it was full-on dark.

"I'll go," I said. "You're a better shot. Cover me with your rifle."

"Good luck, Mr. Watson," he said.

"I just hope Mr. Holmes is in this evening."

I walked toward the house. I could hear music coming from the front room, where a single lamp glowed. Someone was playing the fiddle. But it wasn't like the fiddle music we had up home. The music was slow and strange, complicated. Beautiful.

I went into the yard. After one last look around, I walked up the steps, drew a breath, and knocked on the door.

The music stopped, and the lamp in the front room went out. I held my empty hands out at my sides. In the front window, the curtains moved. They were taking a look at me.

I heard movement inside. A bolt slid back, and the door opened a few inches. A woman's voice said, "What do you want?"

"My name's Watson," I said. "I'm looking for Holmes."

Silence.

I started again, "My name is--"

"We heard you," the woman said.

A long pause. Then the door opened. The woman said, "Slow. Keep you hands where we can see them."

I drew another breath and walked forward through the doorway. Then I felt a gun barrel press against the back of my head. "Keep moving," said a man's voice, and I walked forward. I heard the door shut and the bolt slide home.

The man said, "Stop." I stopped and saw the flare of a match to my right. The woman lit a lamp.

"You armed?" the man said.

"Yes," I said. "A pistol in the back, under my coat."

The woman put the lamp down on a table. I could see her now. Tall and lean with dark hair, she had the look of someone ready for a fight. She took my pistol, checked to see if it was loaded, and aimed it at my belly.

"You alone?" The man said.

"No. One more. Across the road."

"What do you want?"

"Help."

"What kind of help?"

"Jane Darcy."

"Jane Darcy?" he said. "She's at Government headquarters. Everyone knows that. Is that all you want?"

"No. We want to get her out."

"You'd need an army to get her out of there."

"Will you help us or not?" I said.

There was a long silence. The woman gave a single nod. Then the gun was pulled away from my head, and the man said, "We'll see. Get your partner. Meet you around back."

I turned to look at him. He was a tall balding man without a beard, about my father's age. "My pistol?" I said.

He nodded in the direction of the woman. I turned back toward her. She handed it to me, and I stuck it in my belt.

I waited until they put out the lamp before going out onto the porch. Taking a deep breath, I signaled Riley to follow me to the back.

The man took us to the cellar. He showed us a chamber behind a set of shelves. That was our hiding place should soldiers, or anyone else, come to the house.

"I imagine you're hungry," he said. "We'll get you some food. Then we'll talk."

The woman brought us each a bowl of stew, which Riley and I ate quickly. It was our first hot food in a long time.

The man and the woman sat on wooden crates and asked questions. They wanted to know about our militia, about the war, about Jane's part in it. When we told them we wanted to rescue Jane, they looked at us like we were crazy.

"If they were from the Government," the man said, "they'd have a more believable story."

Riley and I kept quiet, waiting.

Finally, the woman said, "We'll have to get a decision from the leadership." The man nodded.

"How do you do that?" I said.

"You don't need to know," the man said.

"How long will it take?" I said.

"It will take as long as it takes," he said.

So much, I thought, for asking questions.

"In the meantime," the woman said, "we'll see what you can do about the way you look."

Riley and I glanced at each other.

"In what we're doing," the woman said, "you never want people to notice you. But everything about you two, your clothes, your hair, and no offense, the way you smell, just screams, 'Hillbilly.'"

"None taken, Ma'am," I said. "But what can we do about that."

"A bath and a haircut to begin," she said. "And we'll wash your clothes."

"What are your names?" I said.

"It's better if you don't know," he said. "Call us John and Mary. What shall we call you?"

"You mean, not my real name?" I said.

"Right," he said.

"Call me Peter," I said.

"Paul," Riley said.

"OK, Peter and Paul," the woman said. "You get some sleep now. We'll start tomorrow."

They went upstairs. Riley and I laid out our bedrolls.

"Whatcha think?" Riley said.

"Not what I expected, but we have to trust them."

"Reckon so."

Soon, I could hear the sound of Riley's breathing. Riley had a talent for falling asleep. I didn't. I just lay awake, thinking about Jane and the strange music.

The next day I had my first bath in a long time. I felt a sorry for Riley, who had let me go first. He would have to use the same water after I was done. But it didn't bother him.

"Up home, my three older brothers always used the bath water before me," he said. "And you're a damned sight cleaner than they ever was."

My clothes were still drying, so I put on some britches and a shirt John gave me. I felt like I was wearing a tent when I went to Mary for my haircut.

She sat me down, and put a sheet over me and cinched it up around my neck. Then she started pulling a comb through my wet hair. "Are you Peter or Paul?" she said.

It took me a moment to remember my false name. "I think I'm Peter."

"So Peter, how old are you?"

"Almost 20, Ma'am. How old are you?"

She stopped combing. "Don't you mountain boys know it's not polite to ask a woman her age?"

"I'm sorry, Ma'am,"

She started combing my hair again and said, "Don't call me 'Ma'am.' It makes me feel old."

"Should I call you Mary?"

"That'll do." She began using scissors to trim my beard.

I let her work in silence for a while. Then I said, "Last night, was that you playing the fiddle?"

"Yes, but it's called the violin."

"Violin? It was beautiful. I've never heard anything like it. What was the tune?"

"Mendelssohn's Violin Concerto in E Minor."

"That's a strange name. The tunes I know are church hymns or have names like 'Wildwood Flower,' or 'Cotton-Eyed Joe.'"

She cut the long hair off my forehead. "It was written a long time ago in Europe. Do you know where that is?"

"Yes, Ma'am . . . Mary. I learned how to read and write in a school we had up home. I liked history. But not much time for reading in the militia. I miss it."

"I'll find you a book."

"Thank you. That'd be nice."

She clipped the hair around my ears.

"Your husband must enjoy listening to you play," I said.

"John tolerates it. But we're not married. We're just together." She paused. "Does that shock you?"

It did, but I said, "It's not my business to be judging."

She went back to cutting my hair. "I was married. My husband was killed."

"I'm sorry. Was he fighting the Government too?"

"No. He wasn't in the Underground. He believed you could change things with words, with talking and writing. He was wrong. The

Government arrested and murdered him."

"I'm sorry."

"Then I joined the Underground."

"You have children?"

"A son." She paused. "We're not going to talk about that."

For a while, we didn't say anything. She kept cutting my hair. Then she said, "Tell me about Jane."

"Well, we told you about the war," I said. "What else would you like to know?"

I expected Mary to ask if Jane really talked with God. Instead, she said, "Is she your woman?"

"No. It's not like that." I felt myself blushing.

"I see. But you're risking your life for her. Why?"

"I . . . we can't just abandon her."

"I understand. But what you're trying to do is impossible."

"Jane did the impossible for us. If it weren't for her, the Government would have our land." I remembered Jane's smile as she stood above Waynesville, watching it burn. And I remembered her screaming in my face, telling me to attack. I pushed those thoughts away.

"She must have been remarkable."

"She is. I'm always afraid. I'm afraid right now. But I don't think she's ever afraid."

She stopped cutting my hair. "My husband was like that. No doubts. A pure faith."

She started cutting again and said, "Who am I to talk? Fighting the Government is hopeless. They're too strong."

"But you're fighting anyway?"

"Yes," she said.

She kept cutting my hair. After a while, she asked about my family and our farm. I talked about that until she finished.

She handed me a mirror with a carved wooden handle. I was surprised by what I saw. My beard was trimmed close and even, and my hair was short, short as Jane's when I first saw her. I felt strange. "So how do you like the new you?" she said.

"Well, I . . . well, thank you."

She was laughing. "Don't worry. You'll get used it. Now get your friend. It's his turn."

I thanked her again and went downstairs to get Riley.

"Damn," he said. "Is that you?"

"Yeah," I said. "Your turn."

Riley stared at me a moment longer and swallowed hard, as though he were nervous. Then, without a word, he got up and climbed the stairs.

I sat on my bedroll and rubbed one hand over my hair, enjoying the strange feel of it. When I was a boy, my mother used to crop my hair real short as soon as the weather turned warm in the spring. For a day or two after, I would rub my hand over the fresh cut hair, just for the small simple pleasure in it, just as I was doing now.

When I was a boy, I thought. That seemed a long time ago. Before the militia, before the blue-eyed man, before Jane, before this. I wondered if any of that boy was still in me. I wondered if any of that boy would make it through what came next.

Late in the afternoon, John came into the house. He pulled something out of his coat pocket and handed it to me. It was a newspaper, just like the ones from before the Plague.

We all went to the kitchen and sat down at the table. The front page had a picture of Jane. Walking on either side of her were two big soldiers. There were shackles around her wrists, and her hair was longer and wilder than I remembered it. She looked right at the camera. There was no fear in her eyes.

It was so good to see her, even this way. She was alive.

Next to the picture, was an article, "Terrorist Goes On Trial." I read the first part aloud for Riley.

> Jane Darcy, leader of the "Hillbilly Terrorists," will go on trial today at the Western North Carolina Military District Headquarters, near Asheville. Darcy, 18, who claims to be the "Messenger of God," is charged with multiple counts of murder, terrorism, using explosive devices, and destruction of federal property. If convicted, Darcy will be executed.
>
> "This self-styled prophetess, this terrorist, will get her day in court," said James Corcoran, head of the Federal prosecution team, "but justice will be done."

I stopped reading. It was just what Hobbes told me they would do.

"What do they mean by terrorist?" Riley said. "That was on the government signs about Jane. Never understood that."

Mary said, "It used to mean someone who attacked innocent people for some political cause. To frighten them. To terrorize them. But now, anyone who fights the Government is 'a terrorist.' John's a terrorist. I'm a terrorist. So are you."

"But they attacked us," Riley said.

"You've got to understand," John said, "facts don't matter. Even the Government's own laws don't matter. They'll find her guilty, no matter what."

"There will be a trial with judges, testimony, and evidence," Mary said. "They might even let her have a defense attorney. It might look like a fair trial. But they will convict her. And they will execute her. They always do."

"So it's all just a big show," I said.

"Yes," Mary said. She was looking at me, hard, and I had the feeling she wanted to say more, but couldn't.

"There'll be more about Jane on the evening radio broadcast," John said.

"Radio broadcast?" Riley said.

"Yes," Mary said, "it'll start in an hour."

John went out to do some chores before dinner. Riley went downstairs. I lingered at the table with the newspaper. My eyes looked at the words and pictures, but I didn't really see. I could only think about Jane. I thought of Jane chained up in some dark room, Jane's fearless gaze in the newspaper picture, Jane closing the eyes of that dead soldier, Jane's touch on my arm, Jane shouting and shaking her head at me, telling me not to do this.

The hour passed and John brought the radio, a black box, into the kitchen and put it on a table. He worked the crank on the side for a minute and then turned a knob on the front of it. After a "click" sound, a man's voice came out of the box. The voice said, ". . . tonight's low will be 52 degrees with partly cloudy skies and a 20 percent chance of rain . . ." The voice went on about the weather, what it would be tomorrow, and the next day.

Riley came upstairs and walked into the room. He gave me an uneasy look. Now, people our age knew about radios. I mean, we had heard old-timers talk about getting music from a radio, but I had only heard the radio Jackson had played for Jane, and that was just for a minute. Riley looked at this one with suspicion, as if he thought it might do something else, like explode.

"Relax," I said, "all it does is make noise."

He motioned me away from the radio. When I was next to him, he said in a whisper, "If we can hear that feller's voice, can he hear us too?" He cast a wary look over his shoulder at the radio.

"There're radios like that," I said. "But this ain't one."

"Sure?"

"Yeah, I'm sure."

He gave the radio another suspicious look and said, "OK."

We sat down and began to listen.

The radio-voice stopped talking about the weather and started talking about factories and food harvests, about tons of corn and wheat, about percentages, records, quotas, and so on. I didn't understand much, but from the sound of the voice, I guessed all this was good news.

The radio-voice started talking about how the Government army was fighting against "terrorists" and "separatist forces" in places like Ohio, Maine, and Miami. Then there was the voice of some General saying it was "just a matter of time," until these places were "fully secure." There was also a report from New York City about the arrest of forty-two "high-ranking members of the terrorist 'Underground.'"

This went on for a while. Riley said, "I don't know much about much, but I think this is all bullshit." Then he apologized to Mary for saying bullshit.

She laughed. "They say this kind of stuff all the time. No one believes it."

I was beginning to wonder whether there would be anything about Jane, when the radio-voice started talking about her. It said pretty much the same things as the newspaper had and listed all the crimes she was accused of committing. Then the voice told us about "recorded excerpts" from the trial.

Then a new voice came out of the radio. I guessed it was the voice of a judge. It said, "Jane Darcy, you have heard the charges against you. If convicted, you may be executed." The voice paused for a moment, and then said. "Jane Darcy, how do you answer? Are you guilty or not guilty of these crimes?"

"Not guilty."

It was her voice. It was Jane. She was alive. I had a picture of her in my mind. She was looking straight at that judge. I was happy, and yet I was full of grief and shame. She was alive, yet she stood before men who would kill her. And they had this chance because I had failed her.

Riley put a hand on my shoulder. Only then did I realize my cheeks were wet. Tears.

"Come on," Riley said.

John and Mary were watching me. I didn't care. I wiped my eyes on my sleeve and tried to concentrate.

The radio-voice came back and talked for a while about how terrible Jane was. The voice made it seem Jane had started the war against the Government because she was a religious fanatic out to destroy all that was decent and good.

Then we heard Jane again.

Another voice asked Jane a question. "You claim to get messages from God. Tell us, does God hate the Government of the United States?"

Jane said, "I don't know if God hates your Government. But I know its soldiers will be driven from our land, except those that leave their bones here."

The first radio-voice came back and called this "a chilling statement by the defendant," and said the trial would continue tomorrow. John got up and turned the knob. A click and the radio went silent. Mary said she would call us for dinner.

Riley and I went downstairs and sat on our bedding without talking. I thought about Jane's voice on the radio. So clear and strong. I wondered what else she had said. Probably a lot. Jane was never one to hold back.

I wondered too, if I would ever hear her voice again. Riley and I might die trying and still do her no good. When I thought about this, a sorrow came on me. It wasn't a sorrow for myself, although I wanted to live. It was a sorrow for Jane, whom I had failed. It was sorrow for Riley, who wouldn't be here if it weren't for me. And it was a sorrow for my people. They needed Jane. But all they had were fools like Winslow and Jackson.

That's what I was feeling when I heard footsteps, heavy ones, coming down the stairs. It was John. He told us to come on up to dinner.

At the start, we were quiet. I sure didn't feel like talking. Mary got out a jug of red wine and poured some for each of us. Then she asked Riley about some story he had told her about his kin. That started Riley telling his funny stories.

I knew the stories, of course, and laughed some, but John laughed very hard. His face got almost as red as the wine. Mary drank only a little wine and smiled at Riley's stories.

After dinner, Mary asked if we would like some music. John and Riley said they would and drank a toast to the violin. I just nodded.

We sat in the front room, and Mary stood to play. Her eyes were closed as she made the strange music. At first, I thought she was playing as if on a stage, playing for many people, people who loved this music. I realized she was alone with the music. The music carried her away from our world of dark and narrow choices.

Her long fingers moved over the strings, and I recalled how those fingers had closed around a pistol aimed at me. Watching her, I knew, knew for a fact, she would have pulled the trigger. She would do what was necessary. For some reason that made me feel better.

When she was done, we clapped and thanked her. She put away the violin and went into the kitchen to clean the dishes and do other chores. Riley and John had one last drink together. Then John went out back to check on his horse. Riley, a little unsteady, went down to the cellar. I went into the kitchen to help Mary.

We stood side by side. She washed, and I dried the dishes. I could see our reflections in the glass window over the sink. For a time, neither of us spoke. Finally, I said, "How did you learn to play music like that?"

She kept washing and said, "Oh that's a long story. If you don't mind, I'm too tired to tell it now."

"I don't mind," I said, but I had the feeling being tired had nothing to do with it. The story was private, like talking about her son.

We washed and dried in silence, except for a few words about where I should put the plates and such.

We finished up. I thanked her for dinner and turned to go.

"Wait," she said and went into another room. I heard her move things around. After a minute, she came back carrying a small book that looked very old. She held it out to me with both hands. I had the feeling it was special to her.

I read the words on the spine. "The Old Man and the Sea."

"Have you read this?" she said.

"No. What's it about?"

"A man who didn't give up."

"Is it a made-up story?"

She smiled. "Yes, but made-up stories can be true."

I didn't know what she meant but was embarrassed to ask. So I just thanked her, wished her a good night, and went downstairs.

Riley was asleep. He had left the lamp burning just enough for me not to trip on him. I was tired, but also curious about the book. So I stepped over Riley, turned up the lamp, and sat down on a crate to read.

In the morning, Riley had to wake me. For a while, I just sat on my bedroll, weary from the night and thought about my dream.

I had been in a boat, like the one in the book, but there was no water. Instead, I sailed skimming the treetops, riding the waves of mountains and ridges, dipping down into the hollows and riding up again on the wind.

This would have been wonderful, but I felt confused and lost, not knowing which way to steer, thinking my destination was one thing, then another, then something else. I was also afraid, because I knew the black-clad soldiers were out there, amid the trees, down in the hollows, over the next ridge, waiting for me in the dark.

Sometimes, Maggie was in the boat with me. I didn't see her directly but only in a reflection from the water around us, which wasn't water, but trees. Yet I could see her, and she was trying to tell me something, something I couldn't understand.

"Feeling poorly?" Riley said.

I must have been sitting there a long time remembering the dream, turning it over, thinking about it.

"No," I said. "Didn't sleep well."

Upstairs, Mary gave us some tea and bread. As we were finishing up, John came in from working outside. He bustled about putting away freshly chopped wood. When he sat down across the table from us, I could see all the good cheer of last night was gone.

"Got a message," he said. "Tonight I take you to your next contact. Be ready to go at dark. Bring your pistols and any ammunition you have. Nothing else."

"Why not my rifle?" Riley said.

"Just do as you're told," John said.

"A rifle will attract attention from soldiers or informers," Mary said.

I could tell Riley didn't want to leave his rifle. It had been in his family a long time, but he nodded.

"We'll be ready," I said.

John got up and went over to his coat. From the inside pocket, he pulled out another newspaper. "More about Jane."

He put it on the table. There was another picture of Jane on the front. Because of her clothes, I guessed it had been made soon after her capture. She sat hunched and chained to a chair. She had the desperate look of a trapped animal, a wildcat.

I read it to Riley. There was some about Jane's trial. Mostly, the newspaper talked about all the terrible things Jane had done. It included what Jane had said about soldiers "leaving their bones here." I guessed they liked that because it made her sound mean and crazy.

"Damn," Riley said. "I didn't know we was mixed up with such a bloodthirsty woman. Lucky Jane didn't cut us up for a thrill." He got up, stretched, and went down to the cellar. He would get his gear ready and then go to sleep. I should have done the same, but for a while, I kept trying to read the newspaper. But my head was too full of Jane to read about factories, harvests, and such. It was all lies anyway.

The day passed slowly. Down in the basement, I checked and rechecked my pistol. For a long time, I lay in the cellar listening to Riley snore, thinking about what might happen tonight.

So I turned up the lamp and read more of the book Mary had given me. For a made-up story, it was very good. The man who wrote it used simple words so it was clear. I could see in my mind what the words said, except for the things about baseball and someone named DiMaggio. But I liked the old man. He was like one of our old men, one of the good strong ones who had not ruined themselves with whiskey and grief, the ones who knew the mountains well, but were always learning.

Though I wouldn't know how, I wanted to be there to help the old man with the great fish. I had trouble imagining being on the ocean in a small boat, floating above all that dark deep water. I had never seen an ocean. Maybe I never would.

The great fish pulled the old man out into the ocean through a night and a day, another night, and into the morning. He brought the fish closer and closer to his little boat. Finally, and he stabbed it in the heart.

It made me think of seeing my father kill a black bear in the woods near our farm. My father shot once, and the bear went down. As we skinned and butchered the bear, we were very happy. The meat would feed us for a long time, and the skin would be very good for trading. My father cut off one of bear's big claws and gave it to me. I kept it to remind me of that day. I remember looking at my father and wondering if I could ever be so strong and skillful. So far, I had never killed a bear. Only men.

The old man tied the fish to his boat and began to sail home. I was happy for him until I read about the first shark.

"Damn!" I said.

By now, Riley was awake, sharpening his knife. He asked what was wrong. I told him something bad had happened in the story. I guess Riley could tell I didn't feel like explaining and he let me alone.

The shark came, and the old man fought it. I put down the book, feeling bad for the old man. There would be more sharks, and the sharks would ruin everything. I remembered Mary had told me it was about a man who didn't give up. But now I knew the old man wouldn't get the fish home. Maybe he wouldn't get home either. I put the book down because I didn't want to face all the bad things.

The sorrow inside me came back.

Then I heard a loud tap-tap-tap coming through the ceiling. This was our signal to hide behind the shelves in the cellar. It meant either soldiers were nearby, or a stranger was coming toward the house. Riley and I moved fast. We hid our things, got in the chamber, and closed the shelves. We stood in complete darkness, pistols ready.

I could hear only two sets of footsteps above us. One set was familiar, Mary's. The other set wasn't heavy like the boots of a soldier, but light. We were safe, and Mary was safe, as long as we remained quiet. I forced myself to be still, but I couldn't relax. The air inside the dark chamber got hot. I began to sweat and thought of the old man in the book. He had gone through so much, and then the sharks came. I thought of Jane, chained up, maybe in some dark and airless place like this chamber. I thought about my parents and Maggie. I had just disappeared. That was bad, but I didn't know what else I could've done. The chamber grew hotter. Sweat rolled down my face. Just when I thought I couldn't stand it anymore, we heard Mary's voice, calling us.

I pushed on the back of the shelf, and we stepped out into the fresher air of the cellar. Mary was waiting for us.

"Sorry," she said. "A woman from down the road. She's lonely and likes to visit."

"Can't be helped," Riley said.

"What time is it?" I said.

"Dinner will be soon," she said. "By the time we're done, it'll be dark." She went upstairs.

The last bit of day light was coming through the kitchen windows when we came up for dinner. John was sitting at the table waiting for us.

"Ready?" he said.

We nodded, and Mary put our food on the table. We ate and said nothing. When we finished, it was full dark.

John put his plate aside. "Get your things."

Riley and I went downstairs and got our pistols. We hid our bedrolls and Riley's rifle in the chamber behind the shelf. When came back upstairs,

John put the lamp out. "Let your eyes get used to the dark," he said. "We'll wait a few minutes." So Riley and I stood still and waited.

I wondered where Mary was, but after my eyes had adjusted, I saw she was sitting in a chair in the kitchen. She was looking at me.

"One at a time," John said. "I'll go first. Wait a minute. Around the house to the front. Across the road. Meet you in the thicket."

Then he went through the back door and was gone.

After a minute or so, I said to Riley, "You go."

He hesitated. Glancing toward Mary, he said to me, "Don't be long now." Then he went out.

I got Mary's book out of my coat pocket and said, "Your book."

"Did you finish it?"

"No."

"Then I want you to keep it."

"Thank you."

I got the feeling you have when you're right on the edge of a cliff, with your toes hanging out into the empty air. If you lean forward just a little more, you'll be gone.

"It's time," she said.

I put away the book and went out into the darkness.

29

John led us south and then east, by way of overgrown roads. Soon there were more houses and more people. But no one seemed to notice us.

After an hour, we came to the edge of an overgrown field behind a large building. John squatted amid the weeds. Riley and I did the same.

A few minutes later, a horse-drawn wagon came around the corner of the building. It stopped, and two men got down. One had a rifle, and the other a shotgun. They stood looking across the field.

John took a deep breath and let it out. "Follow me. Don't do anything sudden."

He took another deep breath, and we all stood up. The men across the field saw us, but they didn't aim their weapons at us. John led us through the weeds and bushes. When we reached them, John said, "Do what they say."

The shotgun man said, "You armed?"

Riley and I nodded.

"Hand them over."

"What?" I said.

"Hand them over," the man said.

"Do it," John said.

Riley and I looked at each other. He didn't like this any better than I did.

"What if we don't?" Riley said.

The shotgun man didn't answer. Then I heard movement behind us, and I knew someone was back there, ready to start shooting.

I looked at Riley and nodded. He looked angry, but we didn't have a choice. Moving slowly, we gave them our pistols.

They had us climb into the wagon. Then they bound our wrists behind our backs and gagged us. Someone put a cloth sack over my head. I couldn't see a thing, and the sack smelled of rotten apples. I felt the muzzle of a gun press against my cheek and heard the voice of the larger man saying, "Lie down." I lay down. The gun pulled away, and he said, "Stay still. Be quiet." I felt something, probably a canvas tarp, cover me. Then the wagon started moving, jolting over uneven ground.

I don't know how long we rode that way. Maybe half-an-hour, maybe more. Every second of it, I had to fight off panic. I kept remembering Hobbes lifting his pistol to shoot me. The dark, the heat, the sickening smell of the sack over my head almost over took me over some edge. I kept telling myself, if they had wanted to kill us, they would have already done it. I kept telling myself it would be over soon. And when it wasn't over, I told myself again. And then finally, it was.

The wagon stopped, and the tarp came off. I felt many hands pulling and pushing me off the wagon. When I was standing, a hand grabbed my left arm and led me up a set of stairs and down what I guess was a hallway. I could hear the rumble of many pairs of boots on wood flooring. I think we went through a doorway and into a room.

"Sit," a voice said, and hands guided me down until my ass hit a chair. Things got quiet. The memory of Hobbes lifting the pistol came again. I pushed it away.

Then someone removed the sack and the gag. The fresh air felt wonderful, and I pulled in a deep breath. It took a few moments for my eyes to adjust to the light. I was in a workshop with carpentry tools, half-completed chairs and cabinets. Sawdust everywhere. Riley was in a chair next to me, his hands, like mine, were still tied behind his back.

Facing us sat a man, perhaps 50 years old, wearing the clothes of a carpenter, but he didn't have a carpenter's hands. He was smoking a pipe and waiting for us to be ready to talk. Patient.

"Hello," he said.

"Who are you?" I said, not expecting an answer.

"Never mind," said the man. "Names are not important."

"You know what we want," I said.

"No, we don't. That's why you're here."

"We want to help Jane," Riley said.

"Do you know how difficult that'll be?"

"No," I said. "And we don't care."

"Tell me about Jane," the man said, "about the war, about how you came to be here."

I explained. Riley threw in details when he thought I had forgotten something.

The man sat smoking, watching us. I felt he knew what we were going to say, but he wanted to see how we said it.

When I was done he said, "You two are a problem. You could be soldiers trying to get inside our organization. But you want to rescue Jane Darcy. That's a suicide mission. So far the Government hasn't been that . . . clever."

"If you ain't gonna help us," Riley said, "we'll do it alone. Let us go."

"No," said the man. "Either we help you, or we kill you. You know too much about us. If you're captured, they'll make you talk."

"But we don't know anything," Riley said.

"You don't know much, but you know enough to get John and Mary captured. And they know a lot."

Riley and I said nothing. I felt the fear begin to leak down through me. We sat in silence until a tap, tap, tap sound came from the wall behind the man. He was being summoned.

The man put down his pipe, stood up, said, "Excuse me." He went through a doorway in the wall and closed the door. Behind that wall, I thought, someone is deciding if we live or die.

I had never been the type to beg God for my life or to try to make some foolish bargain. I hadn't done that when Hobbes was about to shoot me and I didn't now. But I did ask God for Jane's life. God, I prayed, we're all she's got.

The door opened, and the man came out. He sat down and picked up his pipe. "We're going to help you."

I realized I had been holding my breath.

Someone behind me untied my hands.

"When?" Riley said.

"Tonight. We'll get you to someone who can help you."

They let us have a drink of water before putting the sacks over our heads again.

Someone was helping me out of the chair when I heard the man with the pipe say, "Good luck. You'll need it." Then someone led me back to the wagon. As soon as I was under the tarp, I pulled the sack from my head. Riley did the same.

When the wagon stopped this time, someone lifted the tarp, and Riley and I crawled out. I saw we were on a dark little street, but I could hear many people nearby. There was music and now and then a drunken shout. A fat man I had never seen before handed us our pistols. We checked them and put them in our belts at the front.

"Follow me," he said. As we walked away, the wagon drove in the opposite direction.

After a couple hundred yards, we turned a corner and saw a good-sized road. The sound of people and music was much louder than before.

"You won't see soldiers here," the fat man said, "but there are informers everywhere. Don't draw attention to yourself. Just follow me and keep moving."

We headed what I took to be east on the road. There were many people all around us, both men and women. They were standing in little groups, talking, laughing, and drinking from bottles or wineskins.

None of them paid any attention to us except for some of the women who called out things like, "Y'all looking for some fun?" It took me a moment to realize the women were whores. I had heard men talk of going to such women. To me, such things had always been part of another world. Yet there I was, in the middle of it.

We stayed on the road and came to a stretch where the old storefronts were crowded with people. I heard guitar and piano music, as well as loud conversations and laughter. The milling crowds of men and women smelled of whiskey, tobacco, and sweat. A lot of them were crazy drunk. We even had to step over a man passed out on the ground.

As we moved along, I looked at Riley. He smiled and said, "My kind of place." That was Riley.

But I didn't want any part of it.

Just when the crowd started to thin out, the fat man went into one of the old storefronts. Riley and I followed him into a rectangular room. It was dark and filled with smoke, but not crowded or noisy. There were a few tables with chairs along one long wall and at the far end. Along the other long wall was a bar, where men stood drinking, smoking pipes, and talking. Behind the bar was the largest mirror I had ever seen. A few people glanced at us as we came in, but nobody paid much attention. I had a feeling it was the sort of place where folks minded their own business.

The fat man led us to the bar and asked for three glasses of whiskey. The man behind the bar had a blank hard face and a big shiny revolver in a holster on his belt.

When the drinks came, the fat man put some government paper money on the bar. We stood with our drinks and looked around. Riley gave me a little smile and moved his eyebrows up and down. He was enjoying his first whiskey in God only knew how long. I was about to remind him of what Jane had said about drinking when the fat man whispered to us, "Stay here. Don't come until I call you."

Then he walked toward a table at the far end of the room. A black man sat alone with his back against the wall and his hands hidden beneath the table. A rifle leaned against the wall next to him. I watched all this in the big mirror and put my hand inside my coat on the grip of my pistol. The two men talked, and then the fat man turned, saw me watching in the mirror, and nodded.

Riley and I walked to the table. The black man nodded toward two empty chairs. We sat down. I noticed his clothes were neat and clean. He didn't wear a beard.

The fat man turned and left.

I kept watching the black man. He was smiling at us. Then he stood up and grabbed the rifle. He walked to a door in the back wall, opened it, and looked back at us. Riley and I followed him.

He led us down a short hallway to another door. Then he opened it a crack and called out, "Longman. It's me. Everything's OK."

"Come ahead," a voice from outside said.

The black man went through the doorway, which opened to a dark alley behind the building. The smell of rotting food and piss. When I went out, I saw a tall man with a big shotgun. The tall man didn't smile or greet us.

"Let's go," said the black man. He led us eastward along the alley. The tall man walked behind us. After a hundred yards, we turned right and went out to the main road. But we were well past the crowd. Anyone who had been watching us would still be looking at the front door of that bar.

The black man led us east down the road. He was alert and held his weapon ready, but I could tell this was his home territory, just as the mountains had been ours. In fact, they nodded or waved to people we saw along the way. Rather than bars, there were just a few storefronts with traders offering food, clothes, and other goods.

Soon we came to a bridge. We stopped and looked over the side to a much bigger road that crossed below. There were a few of the old automobiles, rusting and stripped hulks, sitting where they had been left in panic during the Plague. But some of the hulks had been pushed aside to clear a path on the road big enough for government trucks.

In the distance, I saw a single bright light moving toward us. But the light didn't shine in all directions like a lamp. It was like a long finger that moved back and forth, searching across the road and the land around it.

The black man said, "A search light on an army truck. Has a .50 caliber. You don't want to fool with that."

"I know," I said. "I've seen what one can do."

He looked at me for a moment, maybe gauging if I was telling the truth. Then he waved us forward, and we crossed the bridge and cut south through narrow deserted streets. Many of the houses along these streets were empty, stripped, and gutted, but a few seemed occupied. As we moved south, I felt hopeful. Jane was south of the city. We were getting closer to her.

The street sloped downhill until it ended where a wider street crossed ahead. Then the black man signaled for us to stop, and get behind some bushes. He went on ahead and poked his head over a rickety wooden fence behind a two-level brick building. He called out, "Hey? Jeffers? You there Jeffers?"

I heard the faint clack of someone working the bolt of automatic rifle, putting a round in the chamber. A voice said, "Who's there?"

The black man said, "It's me, Biltmore. I got Longman and two more."

"Come on then," the voice said.

We followed the black man forward along the fence, through a gate, and to a door on the side of the building. We went through the door and up some stairs to a small room. Longman didn't go with us.

The black man turned up an oil lamp that was sitting on a table and looked at us. "So you two want to rescue Jane Darcy," he said.

"That's right," I said. "You gonna help us?"

He said, "We are."

Riley and I looked at each other and smiled. Finally, I thought, finally.

"Everybody calls me Biltmore," he said. "What'll I call you?"

We told him our names, and I said, "Your name is Biltmore?"

"Everybody calls me that because I lived in the Biltmore House."

"You lived there? Wasn't it a rich man's palace or something?"

"Here's the short version of a long story," he said. "A rich man built it as his house a long time ago. After he died, his family let people come in and see it. For money, of course. People came from everywhere, all over the world, to visit the 'Biltmore Estate.' They had also had a big farm and made wine."

"It must've been something to see," Riley said.

"Yeah, I suppose it was," Biltmore said. "Anyway, when the Plague came my parents were working there. The workers who survived the Plague just started living there, planted crops, kept the looters and squatters away. I was born in the House, grew up there. I lived there until the fucking Government took it away, and ran most of us off."

"So you know the house," I said.

"And every foot of the land around it," he said. "I'm supposed to get you there and back. But it won't be easy, especially after they know your Jane has escaped."

"So how do we do it?" I said.

He laid out a map on the table. "We're here," he said and pointed to a spot on the north side of a river. "We cross this river and go over this big road, I-40, and then keep moving south-southeast until dawn. In daylight, we hide in the woods. After dark, we move up to the house. Longman, Jeffers and some others stage a diversion, a small attack from the east on one of the guard stations. Just make a lot of noise, attract attention, and pull out. That's when we'll go in."

"How?" I said.

"We'll be dressed as soldiers," Biltmore said. "I have uniforms and weapons for us. Your hair and beards are neat enough. We'll need to look and act like the real thing. But let me do any talking. Your mountain accents might give us away."

"This house is a big place, ain't it?" Riley said. "How do we know where to look for her?"

"The army kept some of my people there as workers," Biltmore said. "They've told me where she is."

"Can they be trusted?" Riley said.

"If not, we're fucked," Biltmore said.

"Reckon so," I said. "But how do we get Jane out?"

"We'll go northwest and west, cross the river, and up into these hills," Biltmore said, moving his finger across the map again. "Not many roads there. So the soldiers will have a harder time chasing us. We can hide out there with people I know, then head northeast to the city or northwest to your mountains. Depending. That's our best chance."

"What about to the north, the way we came in?" Riley said. "If you ain't around, it'll be the only ground we know."

Biltmore considered this for a moment. "That'll be hard. The soldiers will figure you'll want to run north, back to the city. All they have to do to stop you is put men on the big road and along the river. With their trucks, they'll get men there before you, even with a good head start."

Riley and I stared down at the map, absorbing all this.

"Once they start looking for Jane," Biltmore said, "it's going to be raining shit. Buckets of it."

Riley and I nodded, looking at Biltmore.

"And boys," he said, "if those bastards catch us, you can do what you want, but I'm saving one bullet for myself."

Riley let out one of his low whistles.

For a moment, I pictured the soldiers closing in and looking down the barrel of my own pistol. Something inside me squirmed. A spasm of loose watery panic. Then I remembered Jane's voice coming through the radio, unafraid.

"So when do we cross that river?" I said.

"Now," Biltmore said.

30

I felt like shouting when I stepped into the cold water of the river. We carried the uniforms, our weapons, and a little food in a pack on top of our heads. By the time I reached the far bank, I was gasping for breath.

We rested and let the cold water run from our clothes for a minute. Then we went up a steep slope filled with dense brush. At the top of the slope was the big road, I-40. When we were almost to the top, one of the Government patrol trucks rumbled toward us. When the light swung our way, we crouched low in the brush and waited for the truck to pass.

We crossed the road, one at a time, at a run. After going down the slope on the far side, we moved up through some hills, across another small river, heading south and southeast. Just before first light, Biltmore scrambled up a little draw, pulled away some brush, and waved us into a small cave dug into the hillside. Once we were all inside, he replaced the brush.

"Make yourselves at home," Biltmore said, sitting on the dirt floor next to the entrance, "we'll be here until dark. Change into the uniforms and leave everything but your weapons and ammo here."

We had more than twelve hours to wait. So we each took a four hour watch. While Biltmore took the first, I tried but couldn't manage to fall asleep. Too many thoughts were flying around inside me. It was actually a relief to stand my watch.

When I woke Riley for his turn, I lay down and tried to sleep again. After a while, I heard Riley say, "Having trouble?"

"Yeah," I said.

"Me too," he said.

That was unusual for him.

"We've come a long way," he said.

"Yeah, I wonder how far since nightfall."

"No, since the beginning, with Jane, and all."

"Oh yeah, a long way."

We were silent for a bit.

"Something I been meaning to tell you," he said.

"Yeah."

"Just wanted to say, whatever happens next--good or bad--I'm glad I did this."

"Good," I said. "Me too." And I had to hold back tears.

"No need to talk of it again," Riley said.

"No need."

"Well, better rest. It's apt to be a lively night."

"Yeah, I'll try," I said and closed my eyes. But sleep never came.

When I saw the Biltmore House, all I could say was, "Damn." I had only seen things like this in the old history books. It stood like a little mountain against the night sky. Bright electric lights shone through dozens of windows.

I turned to Biltmore and whispered, "You grew up there?"

He smiled and put a finger to his lips.

We hid in a clump of trees 30 yards or so from the north end of the building. It seemed the worst place to enter because there were many soldiers around. Two were standing guard, and others were unloading a truck and carrying boxes into the building. There was no choice, but to trust Biltmore.

We sat in the trees until there was a boom and a flash of light from the east. It was followed by the sounds of rifle shots and machine guns. Then there were more booms from the same direction, each louder than the one before. Then the rifles and machine guns continued, back and forth like an angry argument.

At the sound of the first boom, Biltmore came out of the trees and trotted toward the soldiers, his rifle slung over his shoulder. Riley and I followed.

Every soldier, even those standing guard, had turned in the direction of the explosions and gunfire. They were talking with one another. Had any of them looked in our direction they would have seen three black-clad soldiers, rifles slung, trotting up to join the curious crowd.

As we came up to the soldiers, Biltmore asked the nearest one what was going on. The man just shrugged.

The sound of gunfire slowed to individual shots and then stopped. We stood with the soldiers until someone behind us yelled, "Show's over. Back to work!" The soldiers lined up to take a box from the back of the truck. Then they carried the box through a wide doorway into the building.

The three of us did the same. The guards at the doorway didn't even look at us as we passed. We followed the other soldiers down a long hallway, lit with the electric lights. Then we went into a large room, a kitchen with tables, ovens, big pots, heat, and the smells of food. The room was full of soldiers carrying, putting down, picking up, and opening boxes. There were some men in the aprons running around shouting orders. Complete confusion.

We put our boxes on top of a pile. Instead of following the other soldiers back to the truck, Biltmore went out through another door. Riley and I followed.

The three of us walked single-file down a hallway, went down some stairs, and made several turns. We passed a few soldiers coming the other way, but they ignored us, and we ignored them. I had lost all sense of direction and had no idea how to get out of this place.

We kept walking until Biltmore stopped and peeked around a corner. He whispered to us, "This is it. One guard. We walk up. I talk. When I clear my throat, 'Ahem,' Take him. No noise. No blood. Can you do that?"

We nodded.

The guard, slouching by a doorway, didn't pay attention until Biltmore stopped in front of him, with Riley and me to either side.

I was so scared I didn't catch all of what Biltmore was saying. Something about an officer wanting to see the guard right away. I just looked at Biltmore and tried to keep my face blank. The guard was answering when Biltmore cleared his throat, "Ahem."

I slammed my right forearm into the guard's throat and forced him against the wall. His eyes went wide with pain and surprise, and then rage. Riley pinned his right arm while Biltmore drove a knee into his balls, once, twice, three times. The guard's eyes changed from rage to a weak desperation. Finally, his eyelids fluttered and closed. When I took my arm from of his throat, he slid down the wall to the floor. Riley grabbed his rifle.

Biltmore got keys from the guard's belt and started trying them in the lock. He opened the door a crack, looked in, and said to us, "Bring him in." Biltmore held the door open as Riley and I carried the limp body through. We dropped it next to the wall. Biltmore shut and bolted the door.

The room had six metal doors, each with a little hatch at about eye level. It reeked of vomit and old piss. Biltmore went down one side, and I the other, opening and looking through each little hatch. My heart was pounding, but there was a grin on my face. We're going to make it, I thought. Jane's here. In one of these cells.

But Jane wasn't. I found only a soldier, passed out on the floor in one of the cells. A drunk. Stunned, I had no idea what to do next. I turned to Riley and saw it.

The guard was leaning against the wall and raising a pistol. Just as I shouted, "Riley!" the guard fired twice into Riley's back. Riley staggered forward and fell.

Biltmore raised his pistol and fired, hitting the guard in the face. The man slid to the floor leaving a wide smear of blood on the wall.

By the time I got to Riley, he had rolled over on his back. Blood was bubbling up and coming out of his mouth. He looked up at me, confused. Fading. Almost gone.

I stood over him, unable to move.

Biltmore grabbed me, shook me, made me look at him, and shouted, "He's dead! Let's go!"

I still wanted to close Riley's eyes, to say goodbye, but I wanted more to stay alive.

31

Biltmore and I stepped out into the hallway. He locked the door behind us and pocketed the key. He ran to the left, and I followed.

We turned a corner, and I saw an officer come out of a doorway, pistol drawn. Before I could lift my rifle to shoot, Biltmore shouted, "Sir! An accident! We need a medic!"

The officer stopped, uncertain for a moment, and then said, "I'll call." He went back through the doorway.

Biltmore and I followed the officer into a small room. The officer, standing next to a desk, was reaching for what I suppose was a telephone. His back was to us, and he had put the pistol on the desk. Without turning toward us, he said, "Where do we need the medic?"

Biltmore drew a knife, put a hand over the officer's mouth, and pressed the tip against his throat. I closed the door and grabbed the pistol from the desk. I pointed it at the officer.

"Make a sound, and I'll kill you," Biltmore said. "Understand?"

The officer nodded. His eyes were wide open. Fear. I could hear his breath, whistling in and out of his nose.

I heard the sound of many boots pounding down the hallway outside, soldiers getting closer. Then, they passed and turned the corner, receding into the distance. It was quiet again. The officer's eyes had followed the noise as it went past.

"Answer my questions," Biltmore whispered, "and you'll live. Understand?"

The officer nodded again. His forehead was sweaty, and his whole body trembled. His eyes bounced around the room looking for a way out, looking for help.

"Where's Jane Darcy?" Biltmore said and took his hand away from the officer's mouth. I was afraid the officer would cry out, but all he did was gasp for more air through his mouth.

"Answer me," Biltmore said and pressed the knife a little harder.

"Not here," the officer said. "Today they kept her in the city. I don't know why."

Jane wasn't even here, I thought. Riley died for nothing. All of this. For nothing.

Biltmore clamped his hand on the officer's mouth again and moved the knife, slicing deep. The officer looked right at me, very surprised. I stepped back to avoid a spurt of blood. Biltmore lowered him to the floor. Then he wiped his knife and hands on the dying man's uniform.

The officer was making terrible soft gurgling sounds as he clamped both hands on his bloody throat. His legs kicked in little spasms as the blood poured from his neck. I put his pistol back on the desk.

"Quiet," Biltmore whispered. He opened the door, leaned out into the hall, looked both ways, then stepped out and turned left. As I closed the door, I noticed the gurgling sounds had stopped.

This time we didn't run. We walked down the halls, taking several turns and a stairway that went up and up. At last, we reached a landing. We moved to our right down a hall, took a left, and went down another hall. There was a door at the very end. We went through it into a room, and I closed the door behind us. The electric light in the ceiling was off. But a faint light was coming in through a row of windows. The room was crammed with dusty old crates, boxes, and broken furniture.

"Watch the door," Biltmore said. I got behind a pile of furniture and pointed my rifle at the door. I was shaking and breathing hard. Biltmore was behind me at the windows. I glanced at him and saw he was working on a window latch with his knife.

"From here we jump," he said. "Then go northwest to the river." When I looked at him again, he pointed the direction with his knife. "We'll cross and hide in the hills."

He gave up on the latch and moved to the next window. "Fucking rust!" he said.

The thought that I had failed Jane again hit me, and I wanted to drop to the floor. Then the latch gave way, and Biltmore opened the window. No time to think.

"Something happens to me, keep going," Biltmore said.

I nodded.

Biltmore put his knife away, picked up his rifle, and looked out the window. Then he jumped, hit the ground, and rolled. In a moment, he was up on his feet. After I had jumped, we started down the dark slope, moving side by side, a few yards apart, watching for soldiers.

We had just reached the first clump of trees when I heard a loud ringing sound coming from the building, and big lights started going on all around it.

"Shit!" he said.

We went single-file through the trees and bushes, Biltmore leading the way, down the long hill. Before we went across a road next to the river, we stopped and looked around.

"Looks clear," Biltmore said, "Let's go."

We ran to the riverbank. I pushed my way through some brush and stepped off the bank into the river. I was out a few yards, when I heard the rumble of a Government patrol truck approaching fast on the road. Its search light was sweeping toward us. I saw Biltmore wasn't in the water yet. Maybe his coat had snagged on something. Then the search light hit him, and I could hear the truck trying to stop, tires squealing like hurt pigs. Biltmore lifted his rifle. A machine gun on the truck started firing. I saw the first bullets ripping him apart. For just a moment, a bright red mist surrounded him. Spraying blood lit up by the searchlight.

I ducked my head under the water and pulled my feet up so the current would move me downstream, away from the soldiers. The cold water felt like a hand trying to crush me. I forced myself to stay under until I couldn't stand it anymore. Then I let my head come up and, gasping, I looked back. I could see soldiers, lit from behind by the searchlight, standing over what was left of Biltmore's body.

I went down again, and let the current take me further. When I stood to make my way to the far bank, I was well away from the light and the soldiers. Then the shivering hit me, and I had trouble moving my legs. I lost my footing, fell, and felt the rifle slip off my shoulder. It vanished in the river.

It took me a long time to get out of the water and onto the bank through tangled branches and brush. My arms and legs felt weak and clumsy. All I could do was crawl.

I stopped and put my face in the mud. I wept. I wept for Riley and Jane. I wept for Biltmore, a stranger who had saved my life a dozen times that night. Most of all, I wept for myself, because I was alone, shivering in the mud. I wept because I had failed everyone. I wept because it was so easy to weep.

Just when I thought I had come to the end of myself, I felt Mary's book inside my jacket. Sodden, but still there.

I thought of the old man, with the sharks coming for his great fish. I knew it would be sad, but I wanted to know what he would do. I wanted to finish the story. I wanted to live after all.

Then I pushed myself up from the mud and looked up the dark slope. Trembling hit me. I couldn't stand, not yet.

I began to crawl.

32

Around noon, I realized no one was looking for me.

I crawled, then stumbled, then ran up into the hills, always looking over my shoulder for the soldiers. At dawn, I hid in a big thicket. I would wait until dark before moving west again. I was hungry and thirsty, but as the sun rose, the cold in my bones went away.

Although I wanted to sleep, I stayed awake. I dried and cleaned my pistol as best I could, and hoped it would still work. But the hours passed, and I saw no sign of soldiers searching for me. No airplanes circled overhead. Nothing.

I wondered if the soldiers knew there had been three of us. Riley and Biltmore could have killed the guard. After Riley died, Biltmore could have done all the rest. The men who shot Biltmore had not seen me in the river.

Either they didn't know about me, or they were looking elsewhere. Riley and Biltmore had died. Jane was still in prison. But I was safe. I wanted to weep again. Not now, I thought. Save all that for later.

I put my wet boots and Mary's book in the sun to dry. Then I stretched out on the ground, pistol in hand, and slept.

I woke just before sunset and headed west again. I found a stream and drank my fill. Before long, I crossed a big road. On the other side, there were many houses along the smaller roads. I avoided the houses as best I could. In my filthy uniform, I looked like a deserter from the army. Someone might report me for a reward.

I would be safer if I could get ordinary clothes. But I didn't want to use the pistol to take them. I would have to kill anyone who saw me. I wasn't that desperate. Not yet.

So I moved west through the night. An hour or two past midnight, I could see the dim outline of a big ridge to my southwest. I could follow it to get up into real mountains. I might find folks who didn't give a damn for the Government and might help me get back home. But I might not.

I turned north. There would be roads, many houses, and soldiers patrolling the big road, I-40. Going north could get me captured or killed. But John and Mary would help me if I could reach them.

Just before dawn, I crossed I-40. When the sun started coming up, I hid in an abandoned building. It still had some sagging and rusted metal shelves, which once had been piled with food, medicine, or things people just wanted to have. Now the floor was covered with mud, broken glass, and dead leaves blown in through missing windows and holes in the roof. It smelled of old shit and dead animals. I huddled in a corner and tried to sleep with the pistol in my hand.

I would nod off and then jerk awake, certain I wasn't alone and that something had moved. But I went to sleep and dreamt again of sailing in the old man's boat across the ocean of trees. Unlike the last time, no one was with me, and I didn't sail here and there, confused about where to go. I sailed in just one direction, knowing the sharks were all around, knowing I was going nowhere.

When I woke, a large rat was chewing through my britches above the knee. In disgust and panic, I hit at it with the pistol. And I almost shot at the fleeing rat before I got a hold of myself.

It was already after dark, and I had no idea of the time. I was hungry, but it was my thirst that frightened me. How long had it been since my last water? A whole day? Had it been two? My thinking wasn't clear enough to figure it out.

Putting my pistol away, I took a few steps and felt unsteady, as though I was full of whiskey. I wanted to sit down again, but the thought of the rat drove me on.

Outside, I felt better. Thinking about where to go next took my mind off my thirst and hunger. I had to find my way by the shape of hills I could barely see in the dark. Sometimes roads went where I wanted to go, and sometimes I had to cut cross-country. Slow going.

Just before dawn, I saw some clothes hanging on a line behind a house. Someone had been too lazy to take them down last night. I grabbed a pair of britches and a shirt and ran until I found a patch of trees and brush. I changed into the damp clothes, buried the uniform in a shallow hole, and headed out again. Now I could risk daylight travel.

It was sunset when I found John and Mary's house. I knew I had to wait until after dark. So I worked my way over to the thicket in which I had hidden with Riley. In the fading light, I could still see his boot prints in the dirt. It had been just a few days, but it was all as far away and as innocent as my childhood on the farm.

We had hoped we could save Jane. I remember thinking I would save her, or die trying. Well, I had tried, and Riley was dead, not me. He was beyond help. And so was Jane. I knew, finally and completely, what everyone else had known all along. It was impossible. Rank foolishness.

"If it's God's will," Jane used to say, "He'll make a way."

Well, this time God had not made a way, and two good men had died. Jane would die too. I was still alive. I just could not understand why.

Sitting in the thicket, I fell asleep. When I woke up, it was dark. A lamp glowed inside the house.

I tried to stand, but the ground seemed to tilt. I shouldn't have let myself rest. My body wanted to stay where it was. To sleep. I took a step, then lost my balance and sat down on a log.

When I woke up, I was next to the log, my face in the dirt. It was still dark, and the lamp still glowed. Mary was playing her violin.

I crawled to the edge of the thicket and, using a tree, got to my feet. Again, I wanted to lie down, to sleep, but the music reminded me of what I had to do. Once I was moving, it wasn't so bad. I didn't have any problems until I reached the steps. I tripped and fell.

While trying to stand, I realized I had forgotten the code. Was I Watson looking for Holmes, or Holmes looking for Watson? Riley would remember, I thought. Go back and ask Riley. Then I remembered Riley was gone. I began to cry.

Mary told me later that was how she found me. Kneeling on the porch, weeping.

I only remember waking up on a pallet in the basement, feeling cleaner, but still weak. I just stared at the dark ceiling until the door opened. It was Mary, carrying a lamp and a bowl of soup.

"Hungry?" She put the lamp down next to me.

"Yeah," I said, smelling soup.

"When was the last time you ate?"

I couldn't work through how many days it had been. Going to rescue Jane, getting away, and coming here all felt like one long day.

"I don't know," I said. "It was the day after I left here."

"I would've fed you last night," she said. "But you were too upset. It was all I could do to get you to drink some water." She told me about how she had found me on the porch.

I said nothing. I was ashamed anyone had seen me that way.

She helped me sit up, and I ate.

John came in and sat on a crate. He said, "We need to know what happened."

"Tell us everything, so we needn't speak of it again," Mary said.

I told them about the man with the pipe and Biltmore. About getting into the big house. The guard and the empty cells. Riley's death. What the officer had said about Jane not being there. How Biltmore had died and how I had made my way to their house.

I told them what I reckoned they needed to know. It wasn't everything. It would be a long time before I could do that.

"No one followed you?" John said.

"No one," I said.

"If they had followed him," Mary said, "we'd be dead or in an interrogation cell by now."

"I'll be back as soon as I can," John said and went out.

"What about Jane?" I said.

Mary said, "Nothing has changed."

It was another measure of how I had failed. I felt foolish and hollow.

Mary stood up, and started to pick up the tray. Something caught her eye and she smiled. She reached over and picked up the book. "I see you managed to keep this."

"It got wet in the river. I'm sorry I ruined it."

"Oh, it's not ruined. I know how to fix it."

She took the book and the empty bowl and went to the door. "Rest a while. After you eat again, I'll play the violin. Would you like that?"

"Yes. Yes, I would."

"Sleep now." She went out, closing the door.

I slept without dreaming until Mary woke me, one hand on my shoulder. The lamp glowed, illuminating her face. I could smell the rich stew and bread she had brought me on a tray. Outside, rain was coming down hard, pounding on the roof, slashing at the walls of the house.

Sitting up, I ate and felt almost well again. I asked Mary how she had learned to play the violin.

"It's a long story," she said. "But we have time now, don't we?"

She told me the Plague came when she was seven years old. Her family had been wealthy and owned several houses. One of these had been in the country, far from any city. They hid from the Plague there.

They had jewelry, and other things made of gold and silver, to trade for food. That kept them eating for a while, but soon they were like everyone else, getting by on what they could grow and gather.

Mary's mother taught her to read and write using the books in their house. When Mary was a little older, a man who lived nearby taught her how to play the violin.

"His name was Jacob Needlebaum," Mary said. "I called him Mr. Jacob. Before the Plague, he taught music for a living. We paid him a potato or carrot for every lesson." She smiled. "I think we kept him alive with those lessons. Not just the food. Teaching gave him a reason to live. Anyway, before he died, he gave me his violin. That's the violin I play."

"You gave up food for music? Not many folks would've done that. Especially in those days."

"Well, Father didn't like it. He used to have arguments with Mother about it."

"So why did she do it?"

"She said the beautiful things we've created--art, literature, poetry, music--are like a flame we pass from generation to generation. If the flame goes out for even a single generation, it might never be rekindled. The world could go dark forever. It could happen. So easily."

I guess she could tell I didn't understand. "There are the things we do to survive," she said. "And there are the things we do to live."

I guess I still looked puzzled.

"Never mind," she said. "I'll play something for you."

It was strange and wonderful, something from that old world I would never know. As she played, I thought about what she had said. A flame we pass from generation to generation. What about her son? Had she taught him to play? She wouldn't talk about him. I wanted to ask, but I didn't want to cause her pain. Maybe later, I thought.

She finished. I thanked her, and we said good night. When she left, she took the lamp with her, and the room fell dark. I could hear the rain and booms of thunder.

I dreamt of the old man and his small boat again. He saw a storm gathering, moving toward him. The storm hit, and now I was in the boat, not the old man. I didn't know what to do against the wind and the rain and the waves. The weight of the great fish was pulling the boat down into the deep dark water. Lightning showed me the eye of the fish, staring at me, accusing me.

I woke up, breathing hard. It took me a moment to remember where I was, in a house, not in a dugout cave, a thicket, or an abandoned building. There were no rats. I wasn't in the old man's boat. It took a while, but I fell asleep again.

John shook me. "Wake up. It's morning. Come upstairs."

I said I would come. He nodded and went out. I dressed and put my pistol in a pocket of the britches.

Upstairs, John and Mary sat at the kitchen table. When I came in John looked at me without expression. Mary smiled, but I saw trouble in her eyes.

She gave me some tea and bread and asked me how I was. I said I was better. I ate the bread and waited. They were the ones with something to say. They would have to say it. Finally, John did.

"Jane's going to be executed. Hanged. Today at noon. In Asheville. "

Jane's death. It had a time and a place.

"How do you know?" I said.

"The Government has been announcing it on the radio," John said, "They want a big crowd. At the old city hall in the center of town.

I stared at them and tried to control myself.

"There's something else you ought to know," Mary said.

Again, I waited for it.

"They say she signed a confession. They say she's terrified of dying," Mary said.

"I'll believe that when I see it with my own eyes," I said.

There it was. I had to see Jane die.

I looked at Mary and felt she already knew. But I said it anyway. "I'm going." I had to make it real by saying it.

"What good will that do?" John said.

"Maybe if she sees me, it'll be easier for her. I don't know. But I have to do this."

"We can't let you," John said, "If you get caught, they'll make you talk. You'll bring them here."

He was right, of course, but I had to go. I glanced out the back window and saw John's horse was already saddled, tied to a post outside the shed. So I stood up pulled out my pistol. "I'll need that horse."

"Goddamnit," he said. "You'll get us killed."

"I have to do this. I'm sorry."

John glared at me. Mary looked calm. She didn't seem surprised at all.

I kept watching both of them as I went out the back door. Outside, I ran to the horse, unhitched it, and mounted.

Mary came out of the backdoor. She had the book in her hands and walked toward me.

She said, "Just be gentle with the pages."

"Thank you," I said, putting the book inside my shirt. I glanced up and saw John was watching through the kitchen window.

"Be careful," she said.

"I will."

I gave the horse a little kick, and it carried me out into the beautiful summer morning. I was going to see Jane for the last time.

33

I went east, forcing the old horse to keep a quick trot. I did not know how far I had to go, or how much time I had. I remember almost nothing of what I saw along the roads that day. My mind was too full of thinking about Jane.

We had all heard stories about the things the Government did to prisoners. Starvation. Beatings. No sleep. John was right to worry about my being taken prisoner. They could break me. Easily. But Jane? I couldn't imagine her strength failing her. I couldn't imagine her crying, begging for her life when she saw the rope.

My first year in the militia, I saw a man hung. It was some drifter, who had raped and murdered a woman. When we caught him, his clothes were still bloody, and he had the woman's locket. There was no doubt about it.

We weren't any rougher with the man than we had to be. We even made sure he had a final chance to get right with God, but the man just cursed at the preacher who tried to help him. When the man saw the rope, he bucked and squirmed, wailed and cried. We gave a chance to say some last words, but all he did was beg not to die.

I even felt some pity as we sat him on a horse and put the noose around his neck. I felt pity until I noticed again the woman's blood on his clothes. Somebody slapped the horse on the rump, and it ran.

Now, I have seen men die since then, and none went out with less dignity than that piece-of-shit we hung. He was guilty as sin itself. He did not even deny it. He was not sorry for it. He just did not want to get what he deserved.

I didn't care if they had broken Jane, even if she cried and begged before the rope. She didn't deserve to suffer or die. If she was guilty of anything, no men, least of all the Government's men, had a right to judge her.

I didn't care how Jane died. I could forgive any weakness in her because I knew I was so much weaker. But I wondered if Jane could forgive herself. If it came to that, I hoped she could. I said a silent prayer to God, who had been so silent for so long, to help her, to give her whatever she needed.

As I traveled, I saw more and more people on the roads, all moving toward what I took to be the center of town. I followed them. For many, the hanging appeared to be a holiday, a party. I saw some passing around bottles of whiskey and wine. There was laughter and loud talk. I wanted to pull out my pistol and make them be quiet. Instead, I rode on so I wouldn't have to listen.

And there were soldiers along the road, sitting in their big trucks, watching the people go past, waiting for trouble. I tried not to look at them and to keep moving.

Finally, I came to the center of town. There was a four-sided pillar of stone, fifty or sixty feet tall. I had never seen anything like it and wondered what it was for. It stood at the western end of a big open area, which sloped down to the east. There were also large buildings surrounding the area. A couple had been gutted by fire, but most looked like they were in use. Probably by the Government. Soldiers with rifles and machine guns were on top of all the buildings, watching the people below.

At the far end of the area, behind a barrier of barbed wire, stood the gallows. It was a broad wooden platform ten feet high. Above was a big crossbeam. A single noose hung from the center, waiting for Jane.

I tied the horse to a long fence on one side of the open area. From the sun, I judged it close to noon. The field was filling up with people, but there was room in front, close to the gallows. I worked my way forward until I was five or six paces back from the wire barrier and right in front of the rope. I just stood looking at that noose, not quite believing what was going to happen.

Nearby in the crowd, a man started talking about hangings. I couldn't see him, but he sounded like the sort of man who liked to hear himself talk. He went on about the hangings he had seen over the years and the different ways to hang people. He said the fanciest way was to have a kind of door in the platform right underneath the person. When the door opened, they would fall.

"Snap!" he said with a sharp clap of his hands, "their neck gets broke. Dead." He said with a chuckle, "If you're gonna get hung that's the way you want to go."

He said what was more common was to stand the person on a chair or sit them on a horse. When the time came, the chair would be kicked away, or the horse made to run. This was like the hanging I had seen. If the person on the rope was lucky, it was a quick death.

I wanted to ask the man which way they were going to hang Jane. I didn't, of course, but someone else did.

"You'd think they'd do it up right, do it the fancy way, with the door in the platform," said the old man, "but no. They're gonna do her the hardest way. Gonna put the rope around her neck and haul her up inch by inch." This was the way David Winslow had hung those men right after the Plague.

The old man pointed out the rope went up through a pulley and down to a hand-cranked winch. "Yes sir, gonna kill the bitch slooooow." He made some choking sounds, as though the rope was around his neck. Then the old bastard said, "I hope you didn't eat much this morning. You might lose it." He laughed.

So Jane would die the hardest way of all. I looked up and told God, She did everything you asked of her. Everything. And you let her die like this.

There was a rustle of movement in the crowd. Everyone was pressing forward. It was beginning.

Three men came out of the front door of the building right behind the gallows. They went up the stairs single-file and stood in a row at the rear of the platform.

Two were dressed in long black robes. Maybe they were judges. The third man was an Army officer in a black uniform. I guessed he was in charge of their prison.

I was close enough to kill all three of them with my pistol. They deserved to die. But I knew it wouldn't save Jane. And if the soldiers with rifles on top of the buildings were any good, I would be dead before I could empty the pistol.

There was movement behind and below the platform. At first, it was hard to see because everyone around me was standing on tiptoe, and craning their necks this way and that. Then I saw her.

Jane wore a long loose gray dress. Her hair was cut short, shorter than I had ever seen it, and she looked tired and thin. Sick. Her hands were tied behind her.

She walked to the gallows. Then she took the stairs up to the platform, slow, one step at a time, with her head down to watch her feet. I had a feeling she didn't want to trip, to fall, or to give the soldiers any excuse to carry her to the platform. She wanted to show no weakness. They hadn't broken her.

When she reached the platform, she stopped and looked up and out over the crowd come to watch her die. She looked as though she had come onto a stage to sing a hymn or deliver a sermon. To give a performance.

She even had a little smile. But tears flowed down her cheeks.

A soldier took her by the elbow and gently guided her to a spot beneath the noose. She glanced up at it for just a moment, as if it held no special interest, and then looked at the crowd again.

There was a lot of noise, a sort of roar, coming from the crowd. But I can't remember much about it. Perhaps some people were shouting angry things at her. That would be what the Government wanted. The only thing I recall clearly is her standing steady with silent tears.

The officer on the platform stepped forward and called for quiet. Then he began to read something from a piece of paper. It was all about how Jane had been properly tried for this crime and that crime. She had been found guilty and been sentenced "to be hanged by the neck until dead."

Jane never looked at the officer, and he didn't look at her.

The crowd cheered when the officer finished. He let it go on for a while before calling for silence.

I had expected them to give her a chance to say some last words. But they didn't. By now, they knew she would say something they didn't want people to hear.

Three soldiers walked over to Jane. One knelt, tying her ankles together. The other two stood on either side of her as if to steady her. But she didn't need it.

Meanwhile, another soldier starting working the crank to lower the noose so it could go around Jane's neck.

Jane just continued to look out at the crowd, the tears still flowing.

As the noose was lowered to Jane, I stood up straight as I could, and then went up on tiptoe. Look at me Jane, I thought. Please look at me. I'm here.

It was the least I could do for failing her, and for not telling her how I felt about her. I just wanted Jane to know I was here, to know she wasn't alone. She had once told me that nobody ought to die alone.

Jane, I'm here, I thought. Look at me.

Please God, I prayed. Let her look at me.

Then, she did. I believe she found me in the crowd, and she smiled. As the noose was slipped over her head, I believe she smiled at me.

The soldiers made the noose tight around her neck. Two soldiers now worked the crank taking the slack out of the rope. Jane looked up from my face toward the sky and cried in a loud voice, "Oh, God!" Before she could cry out again, the rope was lifting her.

She was on her toes for a moment, and then she was lifted free of the platform. I remember the crowd making noise, shouting angry things, taunting Jane, enjoying her suffering.

Jane's body began a long struggle against death. The rope made it impossible to breathe. Her body shook and jerked like a hooked fish drawn from the water.

I thought of pulling out my pistol and shooting her, ending her misery. I should have, but the plain fact is I did not want to die. I was afraid.

After several minutes of shaking, Jane appeared to grow still with only an occasional twitch. Piss and shit ran down her legs and splattered on the platform. Her face went from red to dark blue. At the end, it was almost black. Her tongue pushed out of her mouth, and her eyes seemed almost to pop out of the sockets. She lost all resemblance to the Jane I had known. The body twisted and swung in a light breeze.

I forced myself to watch it, to witness it all, to remember. Even now, many years later, I can close my eyes and see it. God help me. I can still see it.

Finally, the two judges and the officer left the platform. Some soldiers let Jane down, took off the noose, put her in a tarp, and carried her away into the building behind the platform. I wondered what they did with her. Maybe they just threw her in a hole or dumped her in a river. Maybe they doused her with fuel oil and burned her until there was nothing left. I'll never know.

Then one soldier came up on the platform carrying a bucket and a brush. He scrubbed the spot where Jane's piss and shit had stained the platform. When he left the platform, it was empty and clean, ready for the next hanging.

When I looked around, I saw I was the last to leave.

34

I found my horse, mounted, and let it take me back the way I came. I didn't pay much attention to where I was or where I was going.

It was already dark, and the moon had begun to rise when I got off the main road and started to make my way on the side roads to Mary and John's house.

The horse noticed the sound first. It stopped in the middle of the road to listen. Then I heard it. It was the rumbling whine of an army truck. Coming our way. I pulled out my pistol and got the horse moving again. We crossed a little ditch to one side of the road and went behind some trees.

As the truck went past, I could hear the excited voices of the soldiers. They were all talking at once. I couldn't make out any of the words, but I recognized the feeling. They were relieved. Something had gone better than expected, and none of them had been hurt.

For a moment, I wondered what they had been doing. Then I was kicking the horse into a gallop. I kept my pistol out, although I knew it was useless.

The soldiers had smashed the front door off the hinges. The house was dark. I jumped off the horse, tied it to the fence, and ran up the steps.

John was face down on the floor in the front room. There were several bullet holes in his back. To turn him over I had to step in the pool of blood surrounding him. I closed his eyes. He probably died thinking how I had betrayed them, how I had told the soldiers everything.

I went upstairs, leaving bloody footprints, and checked all the rooms. Mary wasn't there. I went downstairs into the kitchen. She wasn't there either. There was just one place left to look.

Before I went down to the cellar, I sat in a chair and gathered my strength. Maybe Mary was hiding in the chamber behind the shelves. Maybe she had been somewhere else when the soldiers came. Maybe she was safe.

Somehow, I knew she was not.

I lit a lamp and took it downstairs. I opened the chamber. Mary was seated, slumped against the back wall. Her eyes were still open, covered with the blood that had poured down from the big hole in the top of her head. She had killed herself before the soldiers got to her.

I sat down there with her for a long time. It's hard to remember what I thought about. But I'm sure I thought about using my pistol to follow Mary wherever she had gone. I still don't know why I didn't.

Finally, I carried Mary's body upstairs and laid her beside John. I found her violin, Mr. Jacob's violin. I put it by her side and closed her eyes. I wondered again if she had ever taught her son to play so the music could be passed on. Too late to ask.

I stood and looked down at their torn bodies. I wished I had known their real names so I could say goodbye properly. So I could tell them I had not betrayed them. But it was no good wishing for anything, not anymore.

I stood there until the desire to do the next thing came to me. I picked up the lamp and hurled it against the far wall of the room. The glass shattered, and the oil caught fire. In seconds, the entire wall was ablaze.

I walked out the front door. Still tied to the fence, the horse was frightened by the fire and smoke. I had to lead it down the road a little and calm it before mounting. Then I sat and watched the fire until roaring flames came out all the windows.

I turned the horse and rode toward the mountains. Toward home.

When I stopped to rest, I discovered I still had Mary's book. I took it out and turned the pages, turning them gently as Mary had told me. Then I shut the book and put it back inside my shirt.

35

It took me a week to reach the farm where I had grown up, but it was years before I was home.

The day I arrived, dirty, hungry, and leading the horse, which had gone lame, my parents and Maggie asked me what had happened. I told enough for them to know I didn't want to say more. We left it there.

I don't know how other people are, but my people will not pry. They know life is a hard thing, full of sorrow and everyone has their share. And some have more.

The hardest thing I did was writing a letter to Riley's folks, telling them he was gone. I had promised him. I sent the letter, but I don't know if they ever got it.

It would have been harder still to write to Jane's family and tell them just how she died. I would have done it, if I had known where to send the letter.

I went back to work on the farm. That first fall and winter seemed to last forever. But spring came and with it the benefits of Winslow's treaty with the Government. New things, such as radios and medicines, became common in our mountains. I still knew the treaty was a mistake for our people. I said nothing. No one cared what I thought.

After the fall harvest, I married Maggie. I was sad and angry in ways she couldn't understand, in ways I couldn't and wouldn't explain. Yet, she stuck by me, and I seemed to get past the worst of it.

By the next harvest, we had a son. We named him after my dead brother. By the following spring, another child was on the way. I had gotten to the point where I didn't have to shoulder my grief just to get out of bed in the morning. Then one day, I saw a thin gray-haired man walking his horse through my fields. I leaned on my hoe and watched him come. I watched him bring back everything I had tried to leave behind.

"Campbell," I said. I didn't offer to shake his hand.

"We need to talk," he said.

I took him inside. Even though it was a summer afternoon, with plenty of work to be done, I got out my whiskey and poured some in two cups.

"What do you want?" I said.

"To talk about Jane."

"Why? Jane is dead."

"Did you see her die?"

"Yes. And Riley. Others too."

"Tell me how she died."

"They hung her. What else is there to say?"

"You know there's more."

"Do I?"

"Yes, you do."

I glared at him and drank my cup of whiskey in one big swallow. I wanted him to go away. He had brought back Jane standing under the noose and smiling.

Pouring myself another drink, I began to tell him how it was. I didn't tell him how Riley died. I didn't tell him about Biltmore, or Mary and John. He wouldn't care. So I told him about Jane on the gallows, her quiet tears, her final cry, her disfigured face and lifeless body.

He didn't ask any questions. He just listened. Each time my cup was empty, he filled it from the bottle.

When I had run out of words, he said, "We're going to need that story."

"Need?"

"A new war with the Government is coming. We need her again."

"Jane is dead. She can't help anyone."

"Her death was her final gift to us."

I stared at him through the wall of whiskey in my head.

"Unless you tell her story," he said, "she died for nothing."

"God damn you," I said. "God fucking damn you."

"Come back. Tell her story. Jane's story has to be told."

I thought about what that would mean. Telling the story. Reliving her death. Seeing her face turn black again and again. Saying the words until they became just words.

"No, I can't. I'd need this stuff every time," I said pushing the cup away. "You know the story now. You tell some preachers. A good preacher will tell the kind of story you can use."

He looked at the bottle. "You're right."

Campbell went away. I didn't see him out. I just sat at the table for a while until the dullness of whiskey on a hot afternoon started to fade. I got up and drew a bucket of cold water from the well. I drank some and washed my face and neck. I went back in the house and put away the bottle.

Then I went to a trunk and found Mary's book. For the first time since coming home, I opened it. I found my place in the story and read. I read it, turning the brittle pages gently, until it was finished.

The old man fought the sharks, fought with everything he had. Yet the sharks took everything, ruined everything.

I knew how that felt.

Still, when the old man returned home, he got ready to go back to the sea.

I had not done that.

Maybe, I thought, it's not too late.

I took out paper and a pencil stub and began to write this. I decided to tell the story one time, all of it, all the way through. I would tell all the truth I knew about Jane, about Riley, about all the others, about myself, and even about God.

I was angry with God for the way He treated Jane, for the way He let her die. It took me until now to see God had not let her down at all. He had given her exactly what she had wanted.

I thought telling the whole story might give me some peace. And it has. Some.

Just as Campbell said, another war with the Government did come. Once again, I went to fight. And Campbell had preachers tell Jane's story. So everyone knows her story now, and it is told often by our people. Just as we tell David Winslow's story.

A lot of the story they tell is true. Not the whole truth, but true enough, I suppose. There's no mention of me or Riley in the story. That is fine with me. I suspect that would be fine with Riley too.

I'm older now, but at night, I still sit at the fire with the other men. We cook our food and try to stay warm. We tend our wounds and clean our weapons. We tell stories, joke, and complain. We argue about the latest rumors. We try to hide our fears. Nothing, it seems, has changed.

And sometimes, I look out at the darkness and expect her to walk into the light of our fire.

ABOUT THE AUTHOR

Justin Watson grew up on Bourbon Street in the French Quarter of New Orleans. After graduating from the University of the South (Sewanee) in 1979, Justin hit the road. He has been a hitchhiker, a salesman, a deckhand on a fishing boat, a security guard, and a computer systems manager.

In 1996, he earned a doctorate in Religion at Florida State University and taught at FSU, Lafayette College and Le Moyne College. He is the author of two non-fiction books: *The Christian Coalition: Dreams of Restoration, Demands for Recognition* (St. Martin's 1997) and *The Martyrs of Columbine: Faith and the Politics of Tragedy* (Palgrave Macmillan 2002).

Marching As to War is Justin's first novel. *Then the Judgment*, a historical novel about Hannah Dustan (1657-1736) will be released in 2014.

www.ingramcontent.com/pod-product-compliance
Lightning Source LLC
Chambersburg PA
CBHW060945180626
46817CB00004B/1717